THE MUSIC OF DEATH

Full work lights shone onstage where the crew hammered and hoisted and shouted at one another. A musical comedy was booked for the next two nights. Orchestra rehearsals would be held downstairs in a drafty room.

Clarinetist Milton Schring watched the workmen from backstage. He was waiting for Nella to appear. It must be eleven-forty by now, he thought. Where is she?

He looked at his watch, stepping into the light to see more easily. Then he heard the rush of something coming at him from behind. Before he could turn to see what it was a great smashing force struck him in the back of his head. It knocked him to the floor, dead.

THE MURDER SONATA

Frances Fletcher

LEISURE BOOKS ∞ NEW YORK CITY

A LEISURE BOOK

Published by

Nordon Publications, Inc.
Two Park Avenue
New York, N.Y. 10016

CHAPTER I

"In-to-na-tion, in-to-na-tion, please! Watch your intonation!" Exasperated, Milton Schring rapped a pencil on the music stand. His eleven-year-old student was emitting an unforgivable series of honks through a very good Selmer clarinet.

"The clarinet is a very difficult instrument to master," Schring went on more calmly. "Exact pitch is everything. You must *hear* the proper sound before you can produce it. Now, you're doing very well for a beginner—don't get discouraged, Gerry, you'll see what I mean as we go along."

He looked at his watch. "Time's up for today, I'm afraid. Remember, now, *only* the next two pages. No need to try to rush things! Just work on your intonation and your counting. Over and over and over. Be sure you can play aii the notes without breaking the rhythm."

Gerry began putting up his instrument with some alacrity. "Here's your check, Mr. Schring."

"Thanks." Schring folded it and slid it into the pocket of his coat. He had dressed in white tie and tails so he could leave for the concert as soon as the lesson was finished. In the pocket of the topcoat he felt a small piece of paper. What was that, now? He absently unfolded the little white note. He was a neat man; he couldn't remember putting anything in that pocket.

Spread out, the note revealed only two penciled lines:

"If you're serious, meet me in blue dressing room 11:30 tonight." No signature. No name at all. But Schring was only momentarily at a loss.

Ah, the new little clarinetist! He felt a warm glow of satisfaction. Nella Payne, her name was. A delightful girl. Very talented, too. An eager little thing with lively red hair. He had been very nice to her, especially since Millie had gone safely off to Ohio for a long visit home. This Nella had taken up a touch-me-not air, true, but that hadn't fooled him for a minute. He knew he richly deserved his reputation with the ladies.

Catching sight of his own smooth, tanned face in the students' mirror on a side wall, Milton gave himself a dignified salute and then smoothed his wavy brown hair back from the dramatic peak in the center of his forehead.

Well! It would be a nice reward at the end of the evening after that beastly overture was played for the last time. He would take her somewhere glamorous for a midnight supper, and then . . . He turned off lights, locked doors, and drove efficiently downtown to the concert hall in an exhilarated mood.

Life was being good to him of late. There had been some very hard years when he and Millie had married right out of conservatory and—it had seemed immediately—had found themselves saddled with the two girls only eleven months apart. When Millie had insisted that her religion forbade her preventing any future additions to the family, Milton had found his own solution. Using the utmost conservatism in calculating the calendar, he made love with Millie only on guaranteed safe occasions. The rest of the time, he argued to himself, he was free to seek satisfaction elsewhere.

Now that his wife was past the childbearing years, his promiscuity had become a pleasant habit that Milton had no desire to change. And Millie? She didn't seem to mind. Not any more. It was literally years since they'd had an argument about it.

With the girls out on their own and Millie having so much time on her hands, he sometimes wondered if she had a private arrangement or so of her own. On the whole, though, Milton thought not. She was too domesticated. Too satisfied. Or was she?

In the gloomy depths of backstage, musicians in somber black and white drifted about. Nobody had an assigned area, but out of habit most players gravitated to one particular spot or another to open cases, rosin bows, clear spit valves, warm up.

Schring set his case on an upright piano in a corner and put two reeds into his mouth to soak. He looked around.

The whole backstage looped like a horseshoe around three-quarters of the circumference of the main stage and auditorium. All along the outer periphery of backstage were dotted dressing rooms, restrooms, and a couple of plush drawing rooms for VIPs. Below were two basement floors, the lower of them housing the music library and a multitude of storage areas.

At the left end of the horseshoe was the master panel that controlled all the stage and house lights. A balcony booth, high in the rear of the great auditorium, concealed massive spotlight equipment. Backstage could be entered from either end of the horseshoe, but most symphony people came in through the right-hand doors.

Nella Payne stood fifty feet away from Schring. What a pretty girl she was, he thought; medium height, very slender. She had short, dark red hair, not curly but wavy. She was laughing with Zaidee Buskirk.

The two of them had struck up a friendship when Nella had joined the orchestra four months ago at the beginning of the season. The discrepancy in their ages didn't seem a handicap to friendship, nor had the fact that Zaidee was city-bred and sophisticated, while Nella was frankly a small-town girl.

Zaidee, an old orchestra hand who played second violin, was one of Schring's few failures. He had been attracted to her petite figure and honey-colored hair five years ago when he had first joined the orchestra, but her response had been a firm and unmistakeable "no." Her glamour was of the durable variety. She was about his age, or at least in her late thirties, but her shapeliness remained taut and clean-lined. There were undeniable wrinkles in the eye corners, but they had a pleasant trick of dissolving into laugh lines. Rather stung in his pride by her lack of interest in him, Schring had wondered aloud one day why Zaidee had never married.

Bilbo Jones, who had been in the orchestra forever, had explained. "She was married once—didn't you know? Pretty bad experience, I think. Some business-man type who wanted her to give up playing and devote herself to entertaining clients. She tried it for a while, till she found out he expected her to help him get promotions by 'entertaining' his bosses on a one-to-one basis."

Bilbo chuckled. "Zee told him not to be so cheap—if he wanted a call girl, hire one. Took her fiddle and walked out. She didn't ask for, nor get, a dime from that joker, but that's Zee for you; a natural hard-head. Anyway, she's got a fella—he's in the Chicago orches-tra. They meet summers. He comes down here, or she goes up there. She keeps house for her brother. He's a policeman. Their folks are both dead."

A sharp voice hissing in Schring's ear brought him back to the present. "We're truly honored tonight! How in the world did you get here before the downbeat?"

Lottie Williams was at his elbow. She was a second violinist like Zaidee, but unlike her in every other way. Lottie was so ugly that it was hard to believe she wasn't doing it on purpose. Her tongue had a cutting edge even at a whisper, as now, when she reminded Schring of his habit of scooting into place under the maestro's arm. They were not friends, but Lottie had no objection to latching onto Milton as a listener. As long as he was soaking his reeds, she'd have the conversation all to herself.

"Dig the bigwigs conferring," she continued.

Glancing to his right, Schring saw the millionaire Symphony League president, Robert Z. Lyle, talking heatedly with Oscar Manning, the executive secretary. Lyle's silver-topped head towered over the thin, flabby Manning like Mutt over Jeff.

Just seeing them together made Schring's hackles rise. He had only last week won a narrow victory over their plan to dismiss him from the orchestra. Partly, he knew, it had been his own short fuse that had brought the matter to a crisis. But when Manning found that Schring would not accept demotion to assistant solo chair, Oscar had wanted to go all the way and have him fired.

The strongest element of Milton Schring's character was his faith in his own musical competence. It had been simply unacceptable, after five years of playing solo, to step down to second chair merely to accommodate one of Manning's old conservatory buddies.

Why had Lyle chosen to back Manning in such an unfair maneuver? Schring couldn't understand it because he felt sure there was no love lost between those two. But when he—Schring—had refused to step down peaceably for the new man, Freed, and had demanded blind auditions for the principal chair, Manning had given him his year's notice, and Lyle had agreed that Schring must go. It was only by direct appeal to the Players' Committee that Schring had won an audition and thus saved his job and his solo status. Since then,

Manning and Lyle had ignored his existence.

Lottie was convinced that she had solved the puzzle of Manning's and Lyle's relationship. "The big cheese is getting his orders," she chuckled. "What a dog's life he must lead, between Manning here and his wife at home! I hear he doesn't dare brush his teeth without asking her. Must be a total milksop under that frigid exterior.

"Of course," she went on, pursuing a train of thought that endlessly fascinated her, "with all that money, you could furnish quite a doghouse. Wonder how it must feel, having that three-story mansion, and the bay house, and all those furs . . ."

Seeing that Lottie was losing interest in the one-sided conversation, Schring gratefully kept the two reeds soaking until she wandered away. Passing Nella as he headed onstage, he winked and murmured, "See you later."

Though she was a little surprised, Nella rolled her eyes expressively at Milton and nodded. "What's that all about?" Zaidee wanted to know.

"He must mean the overture," Nella said. "It's still tricky, but we're up for it."

She was still in the self-conscious process of settling into the orchestra. Most of the musicians were ten or more years older than her twenty-five. Nearly all had attended more famous conservatories than her own small western one. In fact, several players were middle-aged Europeans who had gained some personal fame before emigrating to America. As she sometimes reminded herself, it was a lot for a country-bred girl to live up to.

Freed was in the chair next to Schring's, warming up. He nodded without stopping the flow of lower-register notes through his clarinet. Studying Freed, Schring thought that his hair was Indian-straight and Indian-black. His cheekbones were high, too, but the skin over them was olive, not ruddy. Well, what difference did it make? They'd probably never be close enough friends for Schring to ask his ancestry.

All through the controversy over the solo chair, Freed had never uttered a word to Schring about it. Every remark he'd ever made to Milton had been some necessary question or comment. The rest of the time he sat silent or played his clarinet, as now.

The players' chairs were filling now. Each musician bent devotedly over his instrument, deaf to anything but the sounds he was making. Just when the cacophony of unrelated runs, trills, chords, phrases, rose to deafening dimensions, the concertmaster, Marcus Belle, brought his violin to the podium. Silence fell instantly. The oboe sounded the concert "A," and violins, violas, cellos, basses picked it up in orderly fashion, tuning meticulously, listening, retuning. Woodwinds and brasses tuned in their turns. Sample, the timpanist, boomed out his intervals, tuning with his foot and bending low over the huge kettles to hear precisely the proper notes.

Tuning up is a show in itself, Nella thought. I love this time before a concert. There's the audience, taking it all in and enjoying it as much as I am. She could just see in the dimly lighted hall some gleams of white shirt fronts and an occasional sparkle from jeweled hair or hands. This has to be more fun than that stodgy British way of tuning up offstage and marching in all silent until the downbeat!

She reached up a long black sleeve for the handkerchief she'd learned to keep handy. Yes, her palms were moist tonight. Nella had begun to believe the older players, who told her you never get over having concert nerves.

Silence fell again, this time serving as a signal to the audience, which began applauding wildly. Trevelyn, the eminent guest conductor, strode to the podium. From the downbeat on, it was a superlative performance. Much smoother than last night. Schring was satisfied with—even proud of—his section's playing of the difficult overture to *Il Forza Del Destino*.

The second piece on the program was what Bilbo called "the stinger"—a composition so modern that Derek John, the orchestra's permanent conductor, would never have gotten the League's permission to perform it. Only Trevelyn's world-wide fame enabled him to sponsor such modern iconoclasts as this composer. Even Nella, who rather liked the piece and found some of its passages quite beautiful, was a little shocked at its blatant experimentation with horns and percussion.

Schring spotted the *Morning Call*'s critic in the second row and winced at the thought of what he would write about in the morning edition. Well, anyway, they had played hell out of it! And the rest of the program was composed of sure-fire favorites. Give the old showman credit—he'd served up a soothing dessert after the strong meat. Maybe he'd get by with it.

By the end of the program, the audience had settled back into enjoyment of their old favorites. They applauded generously, and when Trevelyn graciously signaled a bow for the whole orchestra, all ninety-eight of them could feel that they deserved it.

Schring's watch said 11:00 exactly. Half an hour was time for a quickie at the bar across the street. He moved to duck out past Regal McCord, the stagehand, who was looking awkward in a suit and tie. His union decreed that the hands should wear suits for Symphony performances. Regal sorely missed his battered cowboy boots on Symphony nights.

Not really to Schring's surprise, McCord stopped him. "Say, I need to talk to you about that car of yours."

Milton said innocently, "Is something the matter? It's in the parking garage."

"Not tonight—last night. It was right on the spot where I park my truck. Now, you know I've got to haul heavy equipment in that truck from time to time—lots of times. I've got to have that space clear to park in, so's I can get the stuff into the hall."

Schring said, "Where is it written that that particular spot is your property? I didn't see you moving any heavy equipment last night, anyway. Why would you be moving heavy equipment on Symphony concert nights?"

Both of them kept their voices low; with a guest conductor wandering around, it wouldn't do to let the sounds of friction be heard.

"That ain't the point—it's the principle of the thing! Now, here's what it comes down to: we're going to get this straight, once and for all. You can go to the management—that's Mr. Manning, I mean, in case you're in any doubt—or I will, but one of us is going to get the official word on who parks there."

Go to Manning! Fat chance! Looking closer at McCord, Schring was startled at the knowing look in his little, close-set brown eyes. Why, this clown knew he couldn't, and wouldn't, carry any kind of complaint to Oscar Manning. How much else did he know that was none of his business?

Schring said coldly, "We'll discuss it later, McCord. I'm busy right now." It was merely a face-saver; McCord could tell he had won this round. Milton slipped out for his drink.

Seeing that Freed was at the right-hand end of the bar alone, Schring turned to the left end and joined Toby Whitemore, a bass player, and Evelyn Mitchell, the principal violist. Predictably, there was an argument between them over the new piece Trevelyn had conducted.

"No, seriously, Evvie, there were some very interesting things in there," Toby was saying.

"Garbage! That's all it is, garbage!" Evelyn fumed. She was traditional from top to toe, even to wearing a modified Gibson Girl upswept hairdo. Fortunately, it managed to be outrageously becoming to her soft face.

They turned to Milton, each looking for support for his stand. "Come on, Milton," Evelyn demanded. "Tell him! Statiger is a dangerous lunatic or a complete phoney, and his piece is a collection of show-off noise!"

Taking the stool on Evelyn's side, Milton laid a hand on her smooth nape, pretending to soothe her. "Now, Evvie, don't get excited! After all, Trevelyn doesn't get over here very often. We might not have to play 'Magnets' again for ten years. By that time, maybe we'll have heard so much of this modern junk, we'll think it's good."

He squeezed the back of her neck caressingly, smiling blandly at Toby as he did. Evvie, confused between the caress and her own irritation, slid off the stool and headed for the women's room.

Toby, going to take another sip of his drink, found that he had to unclench his fist first. He scowled at Milton, who was placidly downing a double Scotch. "Someday, Schring," he said softly, "somebody's going to knock your head off for a trick like that."

"Like what?" smiled Milton.

Toby, who was tall and built like a bear, had been cautioned all his life that he must be gentle. "You could hurt someone so easily, Sonny," his mother used to say. "Never, never hit anybody if you can possibly avoid it."

Toby reminded himself of that advice now, and sipped in silence. He was glad when Milton left before Evelyn returned.

14

Backstage again, Schring found the blue dressing room, the last one to the right, deserted. It was a spare, used only during plays and ballet or opera performances. Schring thought it was better not to turn on the light. He waited, sitting on a vanity stool close to the door.

Full work lights shone onstage where the crew hammered and hoisted and shouted directions to each other. A musical comedy was booked for the next two nights. Orchestra rehearsals would be in a downstairs rehearsal room during that time. Voices and noises onstage, projected into the auditorium by an acoustic shell, sounded curiously tinny and far away in the dark little room where Schring waited. Eleven-forty, it must be, he thought. Where was she?

Holding his watch arm out before him, he stepped into the dimly lighted area before the door. If he heard the forward rush of the dark figure behind him, it was the last thing he heard. A great smashing force struck the back of his head. Knocked to his knees, he died.

CHAPTER II

"Come *on*," Nina Oldenberg hissed to her reluctant husband, Julius. She laid a nervous, jeweled hand on his black suit coat and tugged him up as the applause finally died away. "We've simply got to find Trevelyn and tell him how wonderful it was. He'll think we're terrible boors if we don't."

Julius, who didn't care for music in any form, couldn't quite swallow that. "How can he think anything like that? We just spent the whole afternoon listening to him talk and play that damned cello, didn't we? And here we are now at his damned concert. Anyway, he's got a plane to catch. We'd just be in the way.

"That's just the point," Nina explained, leaning against his back to propel him against the stream of people heading for the exits in the rear of the auditorium. "We've made friends with him. Now we have to act like friends. Oh, Juley, I know you're a musical moron and this isn't your bag at all, but just be nice, sweetheart. Just be nice. Tomorrow we'll do something you like."

She slid an arm under his, around to his lean belly, and gave him a suggestive pinch. Julius sighed. He and Nina had a good thing going, and part of it was that they had no illusions about each other. She knew him for a big, dumb, amateur athlete who was lucky enough to have been born into money. Julius' daddy had bought up real estate for the taxes owing during the depression, hung onto it through all the lean years, and now was garnering buckets of gold on rent days. Big chunks of the city bore buildings where he was the landlord.

Nina had beauty and glamour and shrewd social sense. She managed his house, his servants and his family with a graceful hand. If, with the other hand, she conducted one clandestine romance after another, Julius had steeled himself not to know. The trick was never to know for sure; and always to remember, it was a way of life with Nina. None of her flirtations lasted, or meant anything to her.

What was really baffling to Julius was her thirst for music. They found Trevelyn mopping his brown and accepting congratulations from Robert Z. Lyle and several white-haired, jewel-encrusted members of the Symphony League. Watching his flamboyant wife mingle with these prosperous antiques, Julius Oldenberg asked himself for the thousandth time, why? What did she get out of it? Her daddy had left her rich, very rich in her own right, with oil money. What did she want with these fragile old bores?

Nina had two "whys" in her head. One, she frequently explained to Julius. The other, he'd never understand. What she told him was that she needed these people, with their inherited affluence and their easy acceptance of the best things in life as no more than their due. She studied them as one might study books, to understand how to be comfortable with money.

Success in oil had come to her dad four or five years too late, from Nina's point of view. Graduating from high school, she'd been a poor, second-hand-clothes nobody. Even saving up money for a permanent home was a long-time project. She had spent a year as a clerk in a hometown dime store before the big well finally came in.

Suddenly Nina was a glamour girl. She had a new car and was enrolled in the state's biggest university. She had shoes and clothes and belated, but still successful, orthodontistry. She wasn't as successful at the university as she had been all through public school. Her grades slipped to barely passing while she experimented with new cars, new boy friends, and alcohol. Her mother and father, as stunned as she by sudden affluence, had taken an indulgent attitude. Nina needed time to adjust to her new life. That's what they said to their friends when she climaxed a drunken football weekend by a runaway marriage to the quarterback.

Two husbands later, Nina was still adjusting. One real interest had emerged. She had always envied those friends who had been able to buy musical instruments, play in the band, take piano lessons. Now, at least, she could patronize musicians. She was a major supporter of the Symphony League and a most faithful concert-goer.

Trevelyn was quite a little fellow. Nina, whose high heels added four inches to her medium height, stooped a little to kiss the silver bangs on his forehead. "Bravo, Maestro. You were brilliant," she murmured.

"D'you think so?" he asked, with that British air of astonishment that always takes Americans aback. "Thanks so much, my dear. I was just telling Bob, here, about your wonderful hospitality this afternoon." He mopped vigorously at his face. Five tours in America had still not accustomed him to these heated concert halls.

Robert Lyle nodded his head, unsmiling, in a formal greeting to Nina. She touched his arm and smiled easily. "Hello, Robert. Juley, say hello to Robert." She was thinking that Trevelyn might have scored an international first by calling the unbending Symphony League

18

president "Bob."

"Shall we look for that drink?" Lyle urged the conductor. Then, a few seconds too late, he added to the Oldenbergs, "Oh—won't you join us?"

"No, thanks. We'll just speak to a few friends. Where's Milton?" Nina asked.

"Milton . . . ? Oh, yes. No idea. Well, goodbye then."

As they moved out of earshot, Julius asked Nina rather querulously, "Did it strike you that that son of a bitch was snubbing us?"

"Oh, don't mind Robert. He's a moody old thing."

The Oldenbergs sauntered on, stopping now and then to congratulate a musician or greet someone. They had left backstage, and were strolling past little groups of musicians, League members, and visitors in the wide hall that curved gradually to the back exit on the right of the building.

Julius was tired. Stuffed into the dress shoes he only wore for concerts, his feet hurt. He wanted to go find their Cadillac and whisk Nina home. "Listen, Hon . . ." he began.

Nina hated to see him suffer any longer. "Look, Juley," she said, "I just want to visit a little while longer. Why don't you go up to the lounge and have some coffee and a cigarette? I'll come find you when I'm ready to go."

He went, thankfully.

Nina maneuvered herself into a position where she could watch the right-hand exit doors as she chatted with Bilbo Jones. He was explaining that his wife was coming to pick him up when a slim, red-haired girl darted past them and into the yellow dressing room.

"Who was that, a new one?" Nina asked. "She's very attractive."

"New this season. Nella Payne. A nice girl, we

19

think," said Bilbo. "I would have introduced her, but she seemed to be in a hurry about something."

Oscar Manning, walking rapidly, came upon them with his head down, apparently deep in thought. He kept it down for a second or two longer than seemed quite natural. Then he looked up and gave a theatrical start of surprise. "Why, Mrs. Oldenberg! How delightful to see you! The very person I was thinking about!"

"Were you, Mr. Manning?" Oscar was no favorite of hers. Usually, Nina put herself on a first-name basis by the second meeting. Somehow, Oscar Manning never had made the grade. She remained "Mrs. Oldenberg" to him.

"Oh, yes, indeed. I was thinking, you'd be just the person to be interested in a project we're planning . . . in fact, if you could spare me a moment or two right now . . . ?"

"Guess I'd better check my locker before Billie gets here and has to wait for me," Bilbo said, moving tactfully away.

Walking off with Manning, Nina stopped short after a few steps. She had no intention of being guided into a vacant office or dressing room for a prolonged discussion. "I'm afraid my poor husband will be waiting," she began.

"Oh, I know you're going to like this idea," Manning urged. "It's for next fall, actually, or rather the August fund drive. Oh, no, I'm not asking you to be chairman —nothing like that. Mrs. Smallwood is determined to chair it again—and you know how frail she's getting, especially since she was in the hospital for six weeks.

"What we need, basically, is some new, energetic blood," Manning said. He reached a tentative hand toward her, turned the gesture into an eloquent wave when he met her warding look. "New ideas. And we have a pool of willing, highly motivated workers we've never used."

Seeing that he waited for her question, Nina asked, "Whom do you mean?"

His round little eyes sparkled with triumph. "Why, the Symphony wives—the musicians' wives! Who would want the Symphony to succeed more than they do? They live on it—lots of them do. And there they are with time on their hands, nothing better to do."

"I thought—don't some of them play also?"

"Only a handful—not enough to count. We have, I think, four—no, five couples in the orchestra right now. And, of course, some of the wives have other work." Contempt crept into his tone. Manning's wife had never worked a day since they had married, as he was fond of mentioning. "They need the money."

"Well . . . it sounds interesting," Nina said thoughtfully. "Not counting the working wives, or the mothers of very young kids, we might have, perhaps, thirty or forty willing helpers. That's a lot of womanpower. But where do I come in?"

"Liaison, dear lady," Manning said smoothly. He was all but rubbing his hands. "Here we have a chairman of the old aristocrat school. Mrs. Smallwood was born with a silver spoon in her mouth, and is totally unaware that not everybody else was. How's she going to work with a lot of—of working class wives?"

"Very handily, I should think. Mrs. Smallwood never forgets that our players are *artists*," Nina said icily, "and I'm sure she would handle those artists' wives with the consideration and dignity they deserve."

Manning almost writhed. "Oh, but of course, I didn't mean, but—well, she's so *old* . . . ."

Nina relented to a degree. She had never intended to turn down the work. "I've never met the lady myself, but I hear she's a worker. If she does happen to need me or want my help, I'll be glad to work with her."

21

He was painfully grateful. Nina was glad when he finally remembered some duty and scurried away.

Stepping out of the men's room and turning toward the mezzanine stairs, Julius, too, had been waylaid. Out of a clot of long-skirted, fur-jacketed little ladies, the tiniest one emerged with more speed than accuracy, tottering toward Julius with determination. He reached out a hand as much in support as in greeting.

"Mrs. Smallwood!" Looking a foot down into her little old face, he was startled as always at the thin spatter of freckles across the arched, thin nose. Her hand and arm in his big paw felt like a brittle collection of sticks.

"Julius Oldenberg. Haven't seen you since . . . was it when your grandmother died? Remarkable woman, Hattie Lewis. How have you been, child? I was sorry to be ill for your wedding last year. Oh, has it been two years now? Already? Oh, my, but that's not what I wanted to ask you about. What are you doing these days, Julius?"

She peered at him brightly, ready to smile approval if he could say he'd been a good boy. During his boyhood, she had looked at him just like that hundreds of times in his parents' home and in hers half an acre away. Lemonade and cream cheese sandwiches. Delicious. She'd always cut the bread slices in two, he remembered.

He said heartily, "Oh, Miss Verna, I'm not doing anything in particular. We've been on some trips, you know. Nina loves to go places. Just getting settled into housekeeping, you might say."

"For two *years*? Julius! It doesn't pay to be idle, my dear. Work is a habit, a very important habit. Aren't you afraid of putting off beginning too long?"

Good Lord, she'd be calculating his age in a minute. In front of all these old tabbies. Thirty-three probably would seem like a mere infant to her, he thought, but he'd just as soon not have his years totted up in public. She was right; there was too little to show for them. He shuffled his feet.

"Do you remember Tom Padgett, dear? In the bank —our bank, you know? He's losing one of his best young assistants, he tells me. Have you ever thought of becoming a banker, Julius?"

"Why no, ma'am." He'd thought only of an athletic career as a pro football player. When he hadn't been quick enough for that, he'd been content to float along on his trust fund. Why not?

Mrs. Smallwood was telling him why not. She gave him a further homily about the late Mr. Smallwood and his work habits, urged him to call on Tom Padgett without delay, and, squeezing his hand with surprising strength, finally tottered away. The ring of elaborate white coiffures closed around her instantly.

In the lounge upstairs, Julius Oldenberg held a half-filled plastic coffee cup in his hand and surveyed the possibilities. Not many players were left. At a table nearby, however, two women sat, musicians identifiable by their black dresses and by the violin cases at their feet. One was short, squat, and ugly; the other a perfect, fragile beauty. Why not? Julius thought.

"Mind if I join you?" he asked, grinning his ingratiating best.

The beauty spoke. It was such a shock, he almost splashed hot coffee everywhere. Her voice wasn't just hoarse or squeaky; it whined unbearably, like a badly oiled hinge. "Of course. Sit down. I'm Angel Angelo. This is Lottie Williams."

How could a woman, at one and the same time, look like a pensive madonna and sound like Olive Oyl? Ah, well, at least he could look and try not to listen. "How do you do," he said politely. "I'm Julius Oldenberg."

Angel stood up. Yes, indeed, she was perfection all the way down; at least, the dress fell so caressingly that one could easily surmise the sweet curves under it. "Sorry to rush off," she whined, "but my husband has a fit if I'm later than expected after a concert. Nice to have met you."

Dismayed, Julius watched her undulate gracefully away before he turned back to Lottie Williams. She began, "Did you enjoy the concert tonight? Didn't you think, in the overture . . ."

He sighed. This was not his lucky night.

CHAPTER III

Regal McCord, carrying a heavy prop armchair so that he had no visibility directly in front of him, stumbled over the body. His foot tangled with the legs and he went sprawling over it, the chair skidding along the floor.

His right hand, flung out to catch himself, skidded in a wet, sticky puddle. Regal came to his feet, cursing: "Goddamn drunk . . . coulda hurt myself, falling like that! Out to the world, still, even as hard as I kicked him! He must be . . ." He caught sight of the blood on his hand, blackish and sinister in the dim hallway, and trailed off.

Two stagehands ran up to see what the clatter was. With Regal, they bent over the mangled head, face down on the bent right arm. They felt for a pulse, though Schring's hand and wrist were already cold to the touch.

One of them went to find Robert Z. Lyle. He was as composed and handsome as usual but was still carrying the empty drink glass he had absently carried from the Mauve Room where he had been saying goodbye to Trevelyn, who was flying back to London tonight.

Despite his reddish tan, Regal's face paled. His bright little eyes glittered sickly. "Fell right on top of him . . . got my hand all bloody before I . . . goddam! Just a miracle I didn't smash the chair into him, too . . . ."

Usually Regal loved turmoil, gossip, excitement. He was not above stirring up trouble just to enjoy seeing the reactions, but this was too much. He sat down on a prop sofa and wiped at his hand with a handkerchief. Even his lank yellow hair hung listlessly.

Looking like a severely shocked Man of Distinction, Lyle took charge. Work onstage was suspended. He ordered everybody called onstage from the recesses of the building: restrooms, musicians' lounge, dressing rooms where some changed clothes before going home. Most of the musicians had already left, preferring to go straight home in concert clothes.

Nella and Zaidee sat down on the prop sofa next to Regal. Between them was a large, quiet man whom Zaidee had introduced as her brother, Bill Buskirk. Both women had changed from their long black dresses into short street wear, expecting to go to supper with Bill and Ralph Payton. Ralph, a horn player, was as new to the orchestra as Nella was.

Oscar Manning rushed onstage. For once, his slick black hair was tousled as if he had run his hands through it. His round brown eyes looked enormous, sunken. He said, "I've phoned the police. They'll be here in a minute. They said keep everybody here. Nobody's to go home." He glared about nervously, then looked back to Lyle.

"Nobody expects to go home just yet," Lyle said. "We may as well relax. Chauncey, will you make sure that policeman is still outside the stage door? Bob and Willford, stay at the front entrance. Let anybody in, but nobody out." He sat down on one of the musicians' folding chairs that hadn't been removed from the stage set. The others settled down to wait.

Nella asked Regal, "Are you sure it was Milton? I mean, you said he was face down?" She was thinking that it might be any of the other men players, all alike in the black tail coats.

Looking sicker, Regal just nodded, then added

unhappily, "We looked. His face wasn't messed up."

She turned hastily to Zaidee, who had exclaimed as a sudden thought struck her. "Where is his instrument?"

All the musicians in earshot looked around blankly. A small instrument like Milton's clarinet would have been in his hand. He would never have put it in his locker or anywhere else after the concert. Had it fallen with him? It was tremendously valuable; someone should find it.

The second stagehand detached himself from his station directly behind Regal and came back in a few minutes with the little black case. "Who's gonna keep it?" he asked.

"What's that—where did you get that?" Manning snapped.

"Just inside the blue dressing room doorway," the hand answered. "Looks like somebody kicked it. Maybe Regal, or—"

Manning shouted, "You moved it! My God, it might be evidence, and you moved it! Are you crazy? What do you think the police are going to say about that?" He looked as if he wanted to order the hand to put the clarinet back.

Not at all intimidated, the hand drawled, "I sure as hell did, man." He looked about at the musicians circled on the stage. "Who's gonna take care of it?" he demanded.

Nella looked across the stage at Freed, but his head was turned aside. Feeling that a clarinet player should be responsible for Schring's instrument, she said, "I'll hold onto it," and took it, nestling it beside her own case on the sofa. Manning didn't intend to let it go at that, but as he opened his mouth again, a short alert-looking man in plain clothes appeared at stage right. Beside him were two uniformed officers.

Lieutenant Ross was a little quick man with shiny

brown hair and smudgy, tired-looking green eyes. He said nothing until he had taken a long, slow look around the group onstage. His eye lighted on Buskirk. He said in some surprise, "Hi, Bill."

Buskirk had risen to meet his superior officer in the Homicide Division. "Hello, Lieutenant," he grinned. "This is my sister, Zaidee. You've heard me speak of her, the talented member of the family. And Miss Nella Payne, and . . ." he mentioned names around the circle.

Besides all the others, Lottie Williams was there. Silenced for once, she was watching avidly from her folding chair. Howard Freed, quiet as always, sat beside her. The only other musician present was Bilbo Jones. His wife, Billie Jean, sat next to him.

For years Bilbo had been assistant solo trumpet. He was content with the second chair assignment, for he was popular as a freelance jazz trumpet player on the side. Carrying the solo chair responsibility would have been too heavy a load in addition to the jazz work. Bilbo, Billie Jean, and their two teen-age boys were the orchestra's best-liked family.

Bilbo said, "Milton had a wife, Lieutenant. She's in Ohio now, visiting a cousin. The home address will be easy to find, I suppose. Shouldn't someone be calling her? I'll help her about the funeral arrangements, and my wife can meet her at the airport."

"Better let the doc get through first, Mr. Jones," suggested the lieutenant. "Otherwise, Mrs. Schring might have more questions than we could answer. After that, I'll appreciate your helping us with the notification. No young children, then? Good thing."

"Oh, yes, there are two grown daughters," Billie Jean volunteered. "I don't know their married names, though. Millie will have to call them herself."

Ross turned to Buskirk. "Bill, will you go help

Jimmy? He's with the . . . with the doc, out there. Bring me anything you find in the pockets."

As Buskirk disappeared, Manning said anxiously, "Really, Lieutenant, I can't vouch for that man. He's a total stranger to me. Do you think it's wise, having an outsider run around backstage?"

If that amused Ross, he didn't show it. He said soothingly, "Bill Buskirk is in the Homicide Division downtown, same as I am, Mr. Manning. Didn't Zaidee ever mention it? His being on hand is quite a break for me."

Manning said angrily, "Well, of *course*. How was I supposed to guess that! I hope you'll be equally agreeable, Lieutenant, when I tell you that a piece of evidence from the scene of the crime has been willfully removed."

He had all of Ross's attention now. The green eyes glittered as he waited for Manning to explain. "What evidence is that?"

"That instrument there," Manning said, pointing with a flourish to the clarinet beside Nella.

"Is it yours, miss?" Ross asked.

"No, I said I'd keep it for Milton—for Milton's wife, I mean," Nella said.

"Where was it? Did you move it?" Calm as he remained, the lieutenant sounded dangerous.

"No, but I guess it was my fault it was moved," she said.

"It was my fault!" Zaidee said. "I'm the one who thought about it and wondered where it was. I said something, and one of the hands realized that there was a valuable instrument lying around somewhere. He went and found it, and brought it here. That's all."

"Where was it?" the lieutenant asked again.

The hand who had brought the clarinet stepped forward. "It was ten or twelve feet, or more, away from the—Schring," he said. "It was lying inside the door-

29

way of the blue dressing room, behind him. I looked at it good before I picked it up; wasn't no hair nor blood on it," he added.

Nella started violently and stared at the clarinet case. Its finely grained surface was immaculate. Unable to stop the impulse, she lifted it by the middle handle and inspected every inch of the clean underside. When she looked up, every pair of eyes in the room was fastened on the instrument. Hastily, she put it down again.

Buskirk came back onstage. He opened a handkerchief on a coffee table to show the lieutenant what Schring's pockets had contained. Keys, a billfold, a pack of cigarettes, a gold lighter, a folded white paper. Ross opened it and read the message which Schring had rejoiced over a few hours before. After a moment he read it again, this time aloud.

"Does anybody know where this note came from? What does it mean, 'If you're serious'?! . . . anybody?"

Silence. Then in a burst from Lottie, "Get a hand-writing expert! They can tell faking or anything! Get the fingerprints! They can't fool an expert!"

Keeping quiet had been bad for Lottie. Her voice crackled with hysteria. Her short, dark hair frizzed out, as if in sympathy with her inner turmoil. Freed put a calming hand on her shoulder, whispered something.

Ross said, "This isn't writing, I'm afraid. It's very small, even block printing. We'll try with the experts, but I'd guess it has been carefully done to avoid showing any personal characteristics. If you do it slowly enough, there aren't enough personal touches to identify. As for fingerprints, I don't expect much. Any child of five knows from the television how to avoid them."

Lyle looked about uneasily at the restless stagehands waiting at the entrances. "Lieutenant, could we let the hands get on with their work? Whatever happens, the sets have to be changed for tomorrow morning. Perhaps we could adjourn to the big lounge on the next floor below?"

Ross said, "I'll do better than that, Mr. Lyle. Not too much we can take care of tonight, anyway. Buskirk and Able and I'll just get all the names and addresses and a quick statement and let you people go on home for now. We'll pull out ourselves, soon as the crew and the doc are finished."

He started with Bilbo, asking a few questions and taking notes. Sergeant Able, a tall, sandy-blonde young policeman with innocent blue eyes, moved around in the opposite direction. Buskirk started at one of the entrances, checking the stagehands.

Bilbo explained that he had lingered in the hall waiting for his wife to pick him up; their other car was in the shop. "I told her 11:30 would be plenty of time," he explained. "I don't like for her to hang around waiting for me once she gets here."

Lottie, next in line, said she'd felt tired and had had a cup of coffee in the lounge before facing the drive home. What had she done before she had gone upstairs for coffee? Oh, visited with people, she said, waving a hand vaguely. Which people? Oh, various ones. No, she couldn't say for sure which ones.

For a moment, Nella could have sworn Lottie's eyes wavered and her voice changed as she answered with the reason for still being in the hall. Then Nella reminded herself that it was well past midnight. They all were shocked by the—happening—as well as drained from a difficult concert. It would have been more of a surprise if an emotional woman like Lottie had shown no reaction.

Freed, though, definitely had trouble getting his answers together. Finally he said he had gone for a drink next door, and then he guessed he'd spent most of

31

the remaining time "just inside the stage door."

Ross asked impatiently, "Why did you come back after your drink, Mr. Freed? Were you waiting for someone?"

"I was waiting for . . . for Schring. Wanted to tell him something."

"Waiting for Schring? Didn't you go and look for him when it started getting so late?"

"Well . . . no." When Ross still waited, Freed mumbled on, "Actually, I . . . I saw him. Across the street, I mean. But he was with somebody—that is, a couple—well, Toby and Evvie. So I didn't speak to him then."

"Were you waiting for him to return from the bar?"

"No, I saw him go in the door ahead of me. I . . . just wanted a private word. So I waited." Freed set his dark chin sullenly.

Ross started to ask more, and then didn't. He just made a note and went on.

Sergeant Able reached Nella and asked her name and address.

"I'm Nella Payne, P-a-y-n-e. Sixteen-sixty Hawthorne is my address. It's an apartment. Yes, I live alone. I'm not married."

"How was it that you were still in the concert hall so late, Miss Payne?"

The body had been found at 11:45, about forty-five minutes after the concert was over.

"Zaidee and I stopped in the yellow dressing room to change into street clothes," she explained. "We were going out to supper with her brother and Ralph Payton." She explained that Ralph was the musician sitting on the other side of Zaidee.

"You were changing clothes for the whole time?"

"Of course not! We were talking first, to some friends . . . and we had to wait for Sergeant Buskirk to

32

get here."

It all went into the notebook. She couldn't tell at all what impression she'd made on Able. His stolid, unsmiling young face seemed incapable of registering doubt, suspicion, or complete belief. Nella felt the same vague, unreasoning uneasiness she did when a police car pulled up beside her at a stoplight. Next to her, Zaidee recited the same story a few minutes later.

When they all trooped out, dismissed, Ralph tucked her arm into his. Zaidee was on his other side. Buskirk would stay and work on details with Ross, he told them, but the three of them still had to eat. They ordered Chinese food at a little restaurant a few blocks away. Catering to the after-concert trade, it made a specialty of staying open late every Monday and Tuesday night.

Zaidee made a point of ordering two large egg rolls to go for her brother. "Probably the only supper he'll get," she said. She was heavily depressed. "Somehow, it's worse because I never did really like Milton," she said. "In fact, I considered him a jackass with an incredibly swollen ego. But he was a genuinely talented man. You know he was."

They agreed with her. Nella added, "I felt the same way, even though I've only known him a few months. He was a perfectionist about the section—you couldn't get by with a moment's goofing off—but I didn't mind that. That's good for you, keeps you on your toes. It was his . . . his personal attitude I couldn't stand."

Ralph scowled. "I thought he was starting to make passes at you! Why didn't you mention it? I'd have been glad to have knocked his teeth in!"

"That's a good reason for not telling you. Clarinet players can't afford to have their teeth knocked in. Anyway, I could handle him," she said.

Zaidee said, "That was standard operating procedure for Milton with any new female, Ralph. He always had

33

to try a pass or two! Nell knew all about that, didn't you, Hon?''

"Oh, yes, Lottie warned me the first day."

"Count on Lottie," chuckled Zaidee. "If there hadn't been any dirt to tell, she'd have made up some. In fact, I was surprised that she didn't have more to say about this—this horrible thing tonight. I don't mean she'd actually relish anybody's death—you know what I mean—it just seemed to me it would have stimulated her to talk and take an interest. Instead, outside of that one outburst, it looked to me as if she were just plain scared."

"I know exactly what you mean," Nella said. "Come to think of it, she just wasn't like herself."

"Give her time to get used to the situation," Ralph suggested. "By tomorrow she'll probably promote herself to chief investigator."

"Talk about people looking upset," Nella said. "Did you get a good look at Freed? He went almost green when they asked him why he was still in the Hall. What could he have been up to?"

Zaidee said, "Well, I suppose he's in a pretty embarrassing position, when you think about it. Remember, he almost got Schring's solo chair away from him, not three weeks ago."

Ralph said, "What happened to that? Being so new myself, I didn't understand what people were talking about."

"Schring went to the Players' Committee and demanded a blind audition," Zaidee explained. "And he won it, hands down."

"He's that much better than Freed?"

"He is—I mean, was—better than anybody," Nella said soberly.

Ralph asked, "Then why did Freed challenge him to begin with?"

34

"The original proposition to switch principal players was made by Manning," Zaidee said. "Freed is pretty new himself. He may not even have known that blind auditions could be demanded by a musician who is challenged. And, of course, Freed is a competent musician —not in Schring's class, but good."

Nella said, "Who do you think wrote Milton that note? And what kind of 'serious' could it mean? Serious business of some kind? But he didn't have any business but his teaching and his playing."

"God knows," Zaidee said. "I'm still trying to work out the Freed angle. You know, I don't think the poor guy had anything to do with the application for solo himself, except for not being able to say 'no' to Manning. He was just a pawn, I believe, for Manning to use to get rid of Schring."

"But why?" Ralph asked. "If Schring was that good, what difference did it make if Manning disliked him personally? Don't you imagine Manning personally dislikes nine out of ten of us?"

"But he doesn't try to get rid of everybody he happens to dislike," added Nella.

Zaidee said, "Oh, I don't know! I just had a feeling at the time that there was something personal—something deep between the two of them. Anyway, I don't have a clue what that note meant."

"Could mean anything," Ralph said.

Zaidee shuddered. "Let's not think of it any more tonight," she said. "We have to go back there tomorrow morning and rehearse—and you know the police will be there—and everybody will be buzzing about it. It's going to be ghastly."

CHAPTER IV

Little groups of musicians stood about the big rehearsal room downstairs a good half hour before the nine o'clock call, buzzing over the murder. Many of them had heard sketchy accounts of it on the television news or on their car radios. Somehow, it was already general knowledge which ones had been on hand when Schring's body was discovered. In turn, each of these found himself pulled into a group and questioned.

Out of habit, the musicians congregated with people of their own sections. Basses, horns, violas, trumpets, violins, flutes and clarinets chatted nervously or fell into bewildered silences at the same moment.

It was remarkable, thought Nella, how much alike the comments were on Milton Schring. Everybody deplored his woman-chasing and his shabby treatment of his wife. Everybody admired his musical ability. As a viola player who had known him better than most summed it up, "Milton was a son of a bitch, but he was such a *talented* son of a bitch."

Most unusually, Robert Z. Lyle was on hand before the morning rehearsal started. He and Manning ushered Lieutenant Ross into the League president's office when he arrived. Bill Buskirk was with him, as well as Sergeant Able.

Ross's busy green gaze took in the broad walnut desk, its surface immaculate from dust as well as from papers, the elaborate desk chair, two comfortable visitors' chairs. "I hate to turn you out of your office," he said to Lyle.

Manning made a noise between a snort and a sneeze and turned aside with a hand shielding a grin, but Lyle answered with dignity, "That's quite all right, Lieutenant. As a matter of fact, I spend as much of my Symphony work hours calling on patrons and finding new revenue sources as I do on deskwork."

"All right if I use this drawer, and this one?" Pulling them out as he spoke, Ross found in the long top one a gorgeous collection of pencils, pens, and erasers. There was nothing in the other. He suspected the whole desk was quite empty.

"Perfectly all right, sir. There's a private washroom behind that door, and a hotplate and bar facilities behind that one." Lyle gave his social laugh. "Not that you'd be interested in drinking on duty, Lieutenant."

Ross said gravely, "Of course not. Thanks for everything."

At three minutes of nine, the concertmaster rapped for quiet and signaled the first oboe to sound the "A." Nobody had offered to sit in the solo clarinet chair. Marcus Belle, acting as conductor until their regular leader, Derek John, returned from a guest appearance, would have to do something about it.

Embarrassed, Belle said, "Freed, will you take solo for today, please? And Nella, second chair? Thank you." Stone-faced, Freed took the chair into which Manning had recently tried to promote him over Schring's head.

Lyle had excused himself and left the office before the orchestra rehearsal began. Hearing the faraway tuning-up process, Manning said to Ross, "I'd better get along downstairs, Lieutenant. Sounds like they're beginning."

Ross's green stare widened. "Oh, really? I didn't know you actually played, Manning."

"I don't any more. Being executive secretary for the

League is a full-time job. But I like to be on hand during rehearsals. Especially when the regular conductor's not here. They're not above taking advantage of Belle, you see. Need someone who can keep them in line."

"Is that right? You surprise me."

"Oh, they don't deliberately play badly, after all, this is not a junior high band. But they'll goof off, talk when they should be listening. Belle's too friendly with them, too much one of the boys. He just doesn't understand executive responsibility." His manner implied he was an expert on that subject.

"Well, let's just let them struggle along for a few minutes without you, please," Ross said pleasantly. "Sit down, won't you? We didn't really get a chance to go over this matter together last night."

Manning sank into the deep leather visitor's chair and pressed both hands along the sides of his head, slicking back the already well-combed, straight black hair. He said, "That's true. I'd been thinking I'd get by sometime today and give you a rundown on our situation here. Cover the probabilities, so to speak."

"Exactly. That's just what I'd appreciate. Tell me, Mr. Manning, does anybody strike you as a prime suspect? I mean, a long way ahead of everybody else?"

Manning leaned forward, a well-manicured hand waving this away. "No, no, no, no, Lieutenant! That is, nobody I know. What is obvious to me, and must be to everybody who knew Schring, is that this is a revenge job done by one of his women."

"One of his . . . ? He *was* married, wasn't he?"

"Now, I trust we're all men of the world here, so to speak, Lieutenant. I suppose we've all taken a stroll down the primrose path now and then, hah? A man in my position, for example, just has the opportunities rubbed all over him. Wouldn't be in human nature to resist all the time.

"Take yourself, Lieutenant. Married man, are you? No? Why, that makes it even more convenient, doesn't it? *You* know what I mean."

Finding Ross unresponsive to his broad grin and wink, Manning glanced for support at Buskirk and Able. Bill studied him with the profoundest gravity; Able concentrated wholeheartedly on his notebook. After a silent moment, Manning went on.

"But what I'm saying is, Schring overdid it! Chased every skirt that passed by. It was like a challenge to him, meeting a new, pretty girl.

"Well, a man like that develops—castoffs, shall we say? Discards . . . he could handle most of 'em, it seemed, but I guess eventually there was some old gal who wasn't going to be dropped when Miltie got through playing.

"Look how easy it must've been. Backstage door always unlocked before, during, and after a concert. You see a strange female wandering around backstage, what're you going to think? Somebody's wife, sister, mother, neighbor—who cares? It's nobody's business to mind!"

Ross said, "How in the world do you keep from being stolen blind? From your description, anybody could walk in here and take anything that wasn't nailed down!"

Manning grinned. "So take a look, Lieutenant. What isn't nailed down? Stage props, painted flats, instrument cases, maybe, but the instrument and the musician are together, unless it's too big to steal, like a piano or a harp."

"Don't some of the musicians use the dressing rooms, and leave their clothes, I mean their street clothes, in there during a concert?"

Manning laughed. "That sometimes happens, though it isn't supposed to. Each of them has a locker, and is supposed to lock up anything valuable. Some of the girls dress here once in a while, if they happen to have some special reason for doing it. None of the men do—they all dress at home. But if you knew what these musicians make, you'd understand why it wouldn't pay a thief to steal their clothes!"

Manning's hand stroked complacently his beautifully cut, tailor-made slacks. Feeling a surge of distaste for the man, Ross asked rather sharply, "Just exactly what is your function in the orchestra, Manning?"

"I started out just like the rest of them," Manning said. "Small town boy, managed to get hired as a trumpet player. But I soon saw where the money, and the power, are. Management, that's the answer! Oh, yes, I was just one of the players myself once upon a time, and now I'm the guy who knows how to bring them in cheap at contract time, for the management." He put his fingertips together carefully and smiled at the result.

"And in fact, what do your duties consist of nowadays?"

"I hire," said Manning complacently, "and I fire. Of course, there are provisions in the contract as to how that must be done. But as far as the musicians are concerned, I'm the answer man."

"Well, in between hiring and firing, what do you do?"

"Hundreds of things, Lieutenant. You should see my desk. Nothing like this." His plump white hand tapped the empty walnut surface. "Cluttered—piled with work! Schedules, programs, conductors, tours, bookings, VIPs, letters, fund raising, all of it revolves around my desk."

"Well. Let's get down to cases, Manning. Where, precisely, were you between the end of the concert and the time Schring's body was discovered?"

"I! Where was *I*? Why, I never thought . . . oh, of course, probably you have to report to your superiors on exactly where everyone was. Well, let me see."

Manning leaned back and rubbed his chin reflectively. Ross couldn't stop himself from thinking, this is a demonstration of an important executive rubbing his chin reflectively. Damn it, every move the man made came off as a pose!

Eventually, Manning said that he believed he was in the Mauve Room with Trevelyn, the guest conductor, and Lyle for most of the half hour or so in question. "As it happens, though, I was in the little boys' room when Chauncey—the stagehand—came along with the news," he said coyly. "Then I went directly onstage. Mr. Lyle was already there."

Leaning forward again, Manning said, "Don't permit yourself to be sidetracked by routine, Lieutenant. I've told you what must have happened. Take it from me, you have no idea what kind of character Schring was. He acted like a guttersnipe, and guttersnipes are what he attracted. You're going to find this whole crime is totally unrelated to the Symphony. It's just too bad that it's so difficult to get rid of—I mean, to get people like that out of the orchestra."

"Then it's true what I've heard, that you had recently made an effort to do just that—get Schring out of the orchestra?"

Now, at last, there was no posing at all. Manning's round brown eyes could narrow, and they did. "Who told you that? Which one?"

"Does it matter? I simply picked up a rumor somewhere that you were trying to fire Schring, and it hadn't worked."

Manning said, "Don't tell me you can't rig a blind audition! That's what he pulled, to save his job, but all this has nothing at all to do with who killed him.

Internal affairs don't have anything to do with it!''

Ross was getting tired. He snapped, "What is a blind audition, please?"

"Really, I should think the term was self-explanatory," Manning said. "Don't they train you to make deductions nowadays?"

"My department doesn't run on guesswork, mine or yours or anybody's. Definition, please."

"A blind audition is set up so that the judges can't see who is playing when," Manning said sulkily. "So they can judge purely on the basis of good playing—when it isn't rigged!"

"If you figured Schring had cooked an audition, and really deserved to be fired, why didn't you pursue the matter?"

Manning waved the trifling question away. "It simply wasn't that important. I suppose one could say the man was—adequate."

Ross stood up and stretched his short frame. "I believe that covers it for the moment, Mr. Manning," he said. "Have you delivered my message to the concertmaster?"

"Belle's going to have everyone wait for you at the coffee break. I'll see you then." He bustled away, once more the harassed executive.

Marcus Belle, who as concertmaster had to conduct the rehearsals missed by their regular conductor, asked everybody to remain in his chair at the morning intermission. Ross stepped onto the podium and introduced himself. "You have heard by now of the death of your colleague, Mr. Schring. It is necessary for us to ask your cooperation in getting a few facts sorted out.

"Mr. Schring was murdered. Please dismiss from your minds any questions of accidents you might have had. Someone made certain that he would present himself at the desired spot after the concert, and arranged a simple, but very effective, booby trap. We of the Homicide Department expect the full cooperation of every innocent person in bringing this crime home to the murderer.

"My sergeant is handing out paper and pencils. Will you each please list the following information: Your name. Your address. Your phone. What time you left the concert hall last night. What conversation, if any, you had with Milton Schring at any time during the evening. Exact words, please, if you can remember them.

"What person, if any, you noticed talking to Schring at any time during the evening. The exact time, as near as you can remember, that you left here, and exactly when you arrived at your destination. Please list anybody who saw you there."

Able tapped a sleeve, whispered in Ross's ear. Ross said to the group, "Oh, yes. Please state whether or not you have communicated in writing with Schring in the last, say, week. And whether you have handed him any communication in writing from somebody else."

"Fat chance!"Lottie whispered piercingly to her stand partner. "Catch somebody admitting it! Man must be a fool!" The stand partner looked embarrassed. Everybody else, busy writing, pretended not to hear.

Ross had not been home since the murder had been reported. He was too tired to tolerate Lottie's tactics. "Yes, Miss . . . ah, Williams? You had a comment?"

Lottie said, "I said you surely can't expect the murderer to admit making a date with Schring! That's stupid!"

It was difficult to tell whether Lottie was embarrassed or gratified at being singled out for notice. Her face flushed down to the crepy neck, and she glanced about, trying to catch an applauding look.

Ross said, "Miss Williams. Many aspects of a murder

investigation will no doubt strike you as being stupid. Many of them, undeniably, are tedious. Nevertheless, we must go to work systematically and cover all the possibilities. We shall just have to hope that we can survive your displeasure. May I ask, now, why you are not writing down the details we have asked for?''

"I was one of the ones here last night after it happened. The sergeant wrote it all down. You have my information."

"There again, Miss Williams, I must ask for your cooperation. We want a complete file which will include every member of the Symphony. Consider it another stupid police procedure if you wish, but—*do* it."

Ross continued, "As a matter of fact, it doesn't make much sense to imagine that the murderer simply handed Schring the note. If he was going to approach Schring directly, wouldn't he just say the words instead of writing them? And he would hardly have written 'meet me tonight' and trusted to the mail to deliver it on the right day! The only line of reasoning that seems to make sense is that he didn't want Schring to be sure who'd written the note. Thus, he worded it vaguely but made the time and place convenient, so that Schring wouldn't have to put himself out in order to keep the appointment and see who wanted to meet him. The murderer might have slipped the note into Schring's pocket himself. Still, we have to check the possibility that an innocent bystander could have been used to deliver the message.

"So I'm asking you in particular to think about someone who acted as an innocent intermediary, or perhaps someone you saw slipping a note into Schring's pocket."

When the pieces of paper were all collected, Ross asked that those who had been present last night when the body was found should remain after the rehearsal.

44

Nella drifted about backstage during the rest of the coffee break, too restless for coffee. Too late to change directions, she rounded the harp case and found Lottie holding forth to a startled-looking, ethereal Angel Angelo.

Angel had some perfectly respectable first name which everyone had long ago forgotten in favor of the one that suited her exquisite face. Gazing across at her from the clarinet section, Nella loved to watch Angel tuck her violin under her flawless countenance, lift her soulful, incredibly blue eyes to the conductor, and play. She seemed to epitomize all the loveliness of which the string section was capable—until she opened her mouth.

The first time she had heard the high-pitched whine that was Angel's normal speaking voice, Nella had jumped back in shock. Only an unmerciful pinch on her elbow by Zaidee had prevented her laughing, thinking that Angel must be putting it on. In time, Nella came to take both the beauty and the whining as naturally as all the others did. Like them, she learned that if Angel only had one or two specific grievances, she was having a very good day.

"I don't see why I'm the last one to hear any news around this place," she said now. She pushed a curl back of her little pink ear. "And how does that lieutenant know that the ones who stayed late last night are the only ones that know anything? I could tell him a thing or two about Milton Schring's character that might surprise him!"

"I imagine any of the orchestra women he's interviewed will be telling him about the same story on Milton," Nella ventured. "Don't you think so?"

She was saddened to see Lottie nodding and grinning knowingly, as if she, too, could tell a story. Poor Lottie! Imagine Milton pursuing her. That would be the day!

CHAPTER V

Rehearsal went poorly during the second half, as it had during the first. Solo entrances were missed; cues were ignored; accompaniments dragged. Belle, popular though he was, drew resentment as he went meticulously back and back again to sloppy passages and muddy phrases. By the time it was over, tempers were flaring into little brush fires all over the ensemble. Those who could, packed up their instruments hastily and went away.

Seeing that Ross was mobbed at the moment in Lyle's office, Nella wandered into the little cubicle close to the light panel where Regal presided over a coffee urn and paper cups. He made a thriving business of supplying such refreshments to symphony players.

The wiry little stagehand, who had been gossipy and friendly with Nella from the first day she had come to the orchestra, was morose and nervous today.

"Just be glad we're not in charge of the investigation," Nella said. "It's got to be a tough job for Lieutenant Ross and Mr. Lyle."

"Lyle! Much he cares about it," Regal said. "That big dumbbell had to ask me twice before he even knew who was dead. He don't know one player from another."

"Well, try not to think about it, Regal," she offered. "They'll surely clear it all up soon."

"I hope so, miss." He shot her an uneasy glance as he poured her a cup of coffee. "Gave me a hell of a scare, falling over him like that."

"It must have been horrible for you."

"Hell, it was. I stepped right on his leg, you know, and it *gave* . . . couldn't see where I was going, carrying that damn chair, but I know every inch of that backstage with my eyes shut. Just never dreamed of finding a body lying around." His snaky little eyes gleamed darkly at her as he considered for a moment, and then he asked conspiratorially, "Who'd you think done it?"

"I can't imagine anybody doing such a thing. I don't even know what . . . what weapon they used. He was hit, somehow, wasn't he?"

She was sorry she brought it up when she saw the responsive gleam in Regal's eye. Here came the gory details. Even now he would enjoy passing them along.

"Kinda clever, the way it was done. A strong kid could've done it. There was a drop rope hanging loose there, see, and that ladder that's fixed to the wall, in the dark, right next to the little dressing room door. Rope shouldn't of been there, of course, but it was.

"All they done was to tie something heavy to the end of the rope, set it up on the ladder rung, let the little bit of slack in the rope hang down between the ladder rung and the wall, then wait until he came out of the dressing room door and turned toward the stage. Any person's naturally going to turn toward the light—just pull up the slack of the rope—push it off the ladder and let the rope swing it into the back of his head—powie! Didn't even have to be standing close!"

"Well, thanks." Nella backed off, sickened at the vivid picture he had painted.

"Don't you wanta know what they used? The heavy thing at the end of the rope?"

"I . . . have to go now . . ." she was practically running to get out of earshot of the dreadful little man.

"It was a stage weight! One of mine, that I keep in the storeroom!" he bawled after her.

Hurrying around the horseshoe curve of backstage, she almost ran into Lottie Williams. Lottie had just stepped out of the office where Lieutenant Ross was questioning those who had been on the scene last night.

"Are you through in there?" Nella asked. "Is somebody in there now? How do you know when to go in?"

Lottie had built up a head of steam and didn't mean to let a listener get away easily. "They'll call you when they want you," she said. "Not that they'll listen to you, once you're there. What does that man know about musicians? I tried to tell him, we're *different*, you have to use a different approach with artists, you think he listened?"

Frizzles of dark hair shook with her temper. "Insulting, that's what he is. Couldn't see how I spent forty-five minutes having a cup of coffee! Well, of course I didn't! I told him, I was talking to friends, you know how people come backstage after a concert, just couldn't get away without being rude . . . ."

Poor Lottie, thought Nella. She was trailing around backstage tagging into conversations, watching the popular ones being courted by the beautiful people of the city who supported them.

"Is somebody in there now?" Nella asked again.

"They're talking to Freed right now," she said. "You should have seen his face when he went in! Green as a gourd! He can count his lucky stars if they don't tie him into it."

The infuriating thing about Lottie was that it was so hard to let her outrageous remarks lie. Yet if you challenged them, you were playing her game. Exasperated with herself, Nella bit.

"How can you say a thing like that, Lottie? You're practically accusing Freed of the murder! What on earth do you mean by it?"

Lottie chuckled knowingly. "Oh, no, I'm not saying

that he did anything, himself. Not at all! Why, that little pipsqueak would be too chicken to plan a thing like that, all by himself. All I'm saying is, don't the police always go for the one who benefits . . ."

A sudden change came over Lottie in mid-sentence. ". . . so I've got to go home and woodshed, *if* I can get old Prichett to issue me the part. See you later, hon." She moved swiftly away, with an airy little wave.

Turning, Nella saw that Oscar Manning was about to knock on the office door. She slipped past him and found the stairs up to the big lounge.

"There she is," Zaidee said cheerfully, not moving her stockinged feet from the coffee table where they rested. "Been to see the man?"

"Not yet, I'm afraid," Nella said. "He's got someone in there right now. Have you been questioned already?"

Ralph said, "I was first in, I think. He didn't keep me long. Just went over what I was doing while I waited on you girls last night. I told him I'd gotten the music for next week, and sneaked off to an empty room and done a little woodshedding."

"Were you there the whole time?" Nella asked.

"Yes, I thought you could find me by the sound when you were ready to go, so I wasn't watching the time closely. When the hand came to get me, I couldn't believe it was so late."

Zaidee said she was finished, too.

"Oh, don't go off and leave me!" Nella wasn't sure which of them she meant. Both of them answered. Ralph said it wouldn't take long; Ross must be near the end of his list by now. Zaidee said she'd wait, too. Nella felt absolutely limp with gratitude. It was just that Lieutenant Ross had eyes that were so very penetrating, and so very, very cool and green. Like ice. That penetrating stare was examining Bilbo Jones at the moment.

Freed had come out of the office and laid a hand on Bilbo's shoulder to tell him he was wanted next. Bilbo was startled to realize that Freed's hand had trembled just a little.

"Been in the orchestra a long time, haven't you, Mr. Jones?" Ross asked.

"Well, Shad'll be seventeen in August . . . fifteen years, in a month or two, Lieutenant. Since our oldest boy was two."

"Fifteen years. I guess you know most of the musicians pretty well, don't you?"

"That's true," Bilbo said soberly, not liking the prospect of discussing his friends with this stern stranger.

"I'm not going to insult your intelligence by saying that a murder investigation takes precedence over any misgivings you may have about talking about your friends with me," Ross said.

Seeing Bilbo's eyes widen at his mind reading, he grinned. "You can trust us, Mr. Jones, to forget anything you may say, about anybody, if it turns out having nothing to do with the murder."

"Of course. Of course. I'll be glad to help you any way I can. And so will my wife—our other car's in the garage, and she'll be by to pick me up soon, in case you want to ask her anything."

"Now, she was here last night . . . about what time?"

"She walked in just as the hands were running around, calling for everybody to get onstage. She came along with me."

Ross shuffled momentarily through his notes, placed a handwritten one on top. "Now let's see, this says you asked your wife to call you about 11:30, is that right?"

"That's so," Bilbo said easily. "She got here about fifteen minutes late. She's got a good sense of time, herself, but I can't say as much for the kids. They

50

delayed her, and then she had to come through some heavy traffic—there was a football game in town last night."

"So there was. Then I don't think we'll be needing to see her, at least not for now. Let you know if we think of anything to ask her later on."

"Listen, Lieutenant," Bilbo began, fixing his blue eyes on Ross's green ones, "let me say something in general about this orchestra. I don't know how much contact you may have had with musicians before now. I guess, when you first meet some of them, they might look like a fairly mixed-up, neurotic bunch of people. But you see, this is our *place* to be emotional. We've got to feel what we play—and it takes a while, before and after performances—and rehearsals, too, to get back down to a calm level. Actually, when you get to know these musicians, you'll find they're the most normal, nicest people you'd ever want to know."

"Feel responsible for them, don't you?" Ross asked. "I wonder why."

Bilbo grinned and shrugged. "My wife Billie says I'm the one with the maternal instinct. I don't kow, it's just that when you spend years making music with somebody, there's a closeness that develops."

"What did you think about Milton Schring?" Ross asked abruptly. "Did you feel close to him?"

"No, I didn't. Milton could take care of himself, for one thing. I didn't really think much of his lifestyle, and I guess he felt the same way about mine."

"Any ideas about who may have killed him—and why?"

"Isn't there any chanc at all that it was an accident? I heard there was a weight on a rope, and it was pushed off one of those wall ladders. Suppose one of the hands was supposed to put it away, and got lazy and just tucked it out of the way onto the ladder rung. Couldn't somebody have jarred it off by accident?"

"Without the note in his pocket, that might have been a very far-fetched possibility. With the note . . . no."

"All right, then. I don't have a clue who would do such a thing. The worst thing I can say about Milton would be that he was a woman chaser. The best thing would be that he was a first-class musician. What I can't imagine is anybody getting mad enough at him to kill him. People approved of him, or disapproved, according to their own codes of conduct; but why should anybody be *mad* at him?"

"What about a discarded woman friend who might wander in through the stage door? The place seems to be wide open."

"Oh, you'd be surprised, Lieutenant. It's true the stage door isn't locked on concert nights, but just think: there's always somebody, a policeman, on duty outside when the hall is open during a performance. Take a pretty cool murderer to walk in—and out—of a place where she didn't have any legitimate business, right under a cop's nose."

"Could happen, though."

"Oh, yes, it could happen. But then look what she'd have to know: what the blue dressing room was called, since she referred to it in her note. Where the ladder was, with respect to that room. How to get hold of a stage weight. That she could tie it onto the rope without being seen. That he'd be sure to turn toward the stage, instead of the other way, because of the lighting. What time would be safe to have him come there."

"Speaking of that stage weight, how difficult would it be to get hold of one?"

"Not difficult enough, I'm afraid. Regal—McCord, you know—is in charge of the stagehands and equipment. There are a lot of storage rooms at the bottom level. They've got open boxes of weights, things like that, in more than one room. Anybody who knew his way around this place could just go there, choose a weight, lug it up to the dressing room. Do it days in advance, for that matter. I don't know when—or if—they ever count those things.

"Speaking of taking the weight, Lieutenant, there's one idea I probably ought to mention," Bilbo added gloomily. "I hate to make the suggestion, but it's true. We're all so used to carrying our instruments around, and seeing other people do it, that we'd probably never notice an odd-looking thing being carried in some musician's hand."

Ross said, "Wouldn't that lack of noticing apply to anybody? That is, anybody you happened to encounter in this hall? Not necessarily just the musicians, do you think?"

Bilbo cheered up considerably. "Why, of course you're right! Seeing someone carrying something, I wouldn't necessarily say to myself, 'look, that person's not a musician but he's carrying something.' More than likely I'd just never notice it."

"Didn't Schring sometimes bring his girl friends backstage?"

"Outside girls? Never. He kept that side of his life completely away from the Hall. And I promise you, Milton hadn't had a fling with any woman in the orchestra for at least two years. Maybe," Bilbo added honestly, "he would have liked to, but it didn't happen."

Ross was off on another tack. "Mr. Jones, who runs this orchestra?"

Bilbo blinked. "That's a big question. Musically, Derek John, the conductor, works with a committee from the Symphony League . . . ."

"No, I mean, who has the final say over personnel; hiring, firing, who gets the solo chair, who sits in the

53

back. Things like that."

"We've got a pretty good contract nowadays," Bilbo said. "Took us some blood, sweat and tears to get it, too. It used to be that the executive secretary or the League president could say 'off with his head,' and a man would be fired. Over, out, and gone. But not any more. Any player who's not getting a fair deal can go to the Players' Committee and get help."

"Like Schring."

"That's right. Like Schring. But if you're thinking that Freed might have carried a grudge . . . Lieutenant, have you ever heard of anybody *killing* to get the solo chair in a section? I never have. And Freed! He's the most non-violent character I've met in years."

"What about Manning? He must have lost considerable face when he wanted to fire Schring and couldn't do it."

Bilbo spread empty palms to Ross. "Again, is that something a sane man would kill about? Believe me, Manning may be the world's most obnoxious management fink, and a petty tyrannical little jerk on top of that, but he's sane, all right. He's so sharp he controls the very cream of the legitimate music jobs in this whole area. That means he's got contacts, and he's keeping a lot of first-class people impressed."

"Really?" Ross's eyebrows shot up. "His charm seems to have eluded me."

"That's because you aren't useful to him, and you aren't in a position to do anything for him," Bilbo said. "You'd have noticed the charm, all right, if Manning could have gained anything by turning it on."

"The person I thought was really the executive type, and probably had a big potential for winning friends and influencing people, was Robert Lyle," Ross said.

"I know. He impresses you that way at first. And yet, it's hard to pin down. We don't see much of Lyle in

54

ordinary times. Oh, he comes into the office fairly regularly, but usually when we're rehearsing. It's hard to say how much voice in the management he really has. None in the musical decisions, I know that. He's strictly an ex-athlete. Tennis. But his wife is crazy about the Symphony, and she's the one with the moneybags, so they say."

Ross nodded. "That's interesting. Now, what about this talky woman, the aggressive one—Lottie Williams? How did she get along with Schring? Any particular bad feeling between them?"

Bilbo was shocked. "Oh, no Lieutenant! Lottie doesn't mean anything by those outbursts of hers. She's just naturally the hysterical type. Low boiling point, you know, but she would never harm a fly, really. I'm sure Milton wasn't fond of her, and she definitely is the type to disapprove of him, but I can't remember any specific incidents at all."

Ross smiled. "It's surprising to a policeman when somebody says, 'Oh, so-and-so's just hysterical, you know, but harmless.' Don't you know that over half the homicides in the country are committed by persons in various stages of hysteria?"

"Well, yes, but does that apply to this crime? At least part of it had to be planned in cold blood, didn't it? The note, and the rope, too?"

"You've got a point there. And the very attractive lady, is her name really Angel? What's the verdict on her?"

"Angel . . . no, I can't remember. She has some other first name, but I guess we've all forgotten it." Bilbo grinned. "I feel safe in offering you a guarantee, Lieutenant, that Angel Angelo had nothing to do with this crime. Listen to her talk for five minutes and you'll know why I say that. If anything, any tiny little thing, bothers Mrs. Angelo, the whole orchestra hears her complaining about it. She couldn't keep a grievance to herself long enough to get worked up about it."

Ross said, "So, to sum it up, Mr. Jones, you can't give us any guess at all about the killer?"

"A killer . . . in the orchestra." Bilbo was pained, and looked it. "I'd tell you like a shot, if I suspected anybody. It's like being told we have a cancer growing among us. I just can't comprehend it."

CHAPTER VI

Manning, looking more harassed than usual, bounded into the lounge, flinging Nella a *"There* you are!"* as if she had missed an appointment.

"Were you looking for me?"

"Mr. Lyle and Lieutenant Ross are. Waiting for you in the office." Manning always took care to address Lyle with a loud and breezy "Bob," but he made it a point to refer to him to the musicians as "Mr. Lyle."

Manning's sharp tone was new to Nella. Before today, he had been positively overflowing with little pats on the back and kindly platitudes. She was well aware that he was the most powerful music booker in town for the type of work most symphony musicians needed. He controlled most of the outside-Symphony jobs that people like Nella might be called for. No doubt, she thought, that was why he'd expected her to react more agreeably when he'd made a pass at her last night.

Too bad, she thought. I've annoyed the great man. No more outside jobs for Nella. Well, it didn't make much difference, really, whether Manning became angry with her today or soon. It was inevitable that sooner or later, as she kept refusing to play by his rules, she would be struck off his list of clarinetists to call for work.

For Nella, living alone, her Symphony income barely covered a modest apartment in a somewhat run-down neighborhood. She drove a six-year-old small car.

Home-cooked hamburgers made up a big part of her diet.

She had begun building a private teaching practice. Already she had three students and hoped for ten. Next year she might take one of the part-time teaching jobs offered by the city's sprawling school district. One way or another, she could be independent of Oscar Manning, and she meant to stay that way.

Lieutenant Ross greeted her courteously. "Now, let's see, you're new in the orchestra this season, aren't you? What, exactly, were your relations with Mr. Schring?"

"He was very helpful to me," Nella said truthfully. "He was demanding as a second leader, but I think we all appreciated that. It kept us up to the mark."

She couldn't help glancing at Lyle, who was seated on a leather sofa to her right, as she added, "He was an excellent musician, you know."

Ross followed her glance at Lyle. He would have preferred to conduct this interview privately, like the others, but could hardly object when Lyle had walked in unexpectedly a few minutes earlier. He sat on the sofa, apparently absorbed in some papers he was glancing over.

"So I understand," Ross said to Nella. He twirled half around in the roomy padded swivel chair that matched Lyle's desk. His bony face seemed to lengthen with discomfort as he went on, "What I had in mind was more—ah, personal relations. Was he friendly?"

Apparently Ross had heard some gossip about Schring's extra attentions to her. Nella decided she had better be blunt and bring the matter out in the open.

"Well, yes. As a matter of fact, I was wondering if he was trying to be a bit flirtatious. Nothing serious, I'm sure. He was married, you know." She smiled. "I had been told it was his standard operating procedure with new female personnel. I just kept out of his way unless

58

other people were with me."

"Is that so? Did you not plan to meet him after the concert last night? That note in his pocket might easily bear a romantic interpretation."

Her copper hair swung about her face as she shook her head vigorously. "I know nothing about that note. I never wrote a line to Milton Schring for any reason."

"Ah." Ross's slender frame pushed back in the chair as he tried to piece things together. Now he could relax and settle a few tedious details. A tactic? Nella let herself lean back also, but remained alert.

He pounced. "Miss Buskirk admitted that she waited for you in the dressing room—the main one, I understand—for fifteen or twenty minutes after the concert. Where were you during that time?"

Her fingers were twisting and untwisting the catch on her purse. Suddenly aware of her actions, she forced a self-conscious smile.

"I . . . don't know if I can remember, exactly. Was it that long? Mr. Manning took me in to meet the guest conductor, for one thing."

"How long were you there?"

Lyle boomed unexpectedly, "Five minutes." When both of them turned to look at him, he sat on the sofa, still as a Buddha.

"Oh, yes, Mr. Lyle was with him."

"And after you left them?"

"Why, there are always people around. They come backstage to talk after a concert . . . I don't know, really . . ." How weak it sounded! But she couldn't bring herself to recount for Ross and Lyle the sordid little struggle in a dark corner to which Manning, suddenly amorous, had subjected her. How long had it taken her to break loose and dart away?

How could she go into all that, right after she'd admitted that Schring hadn't been able to keep his hands to himself. They'd put her down as a self-deluding crackpot, a wishful-thinking nympho. And yet, Manning and Schring probably behaved more in keeping with today's "new" morality than she did. Who wasn't promiscuous these days? Nella had been called a prude so often she had come to accept it. All right, she had decided back in her conservatory days, so I'm a prude. Abnormal. A freak. I'm not ready to roll in the hay with any fellow who buys me a cup of coffee. Fine. Let it be an advantage to me. I'll have more time to practice! And someday, some wonderful prudish man will come along, and we'll get married and have a lot of little prudes of our own.

The pale green eyes were icier than ever. "Can't account for maybe fifteen minutes of time? Just talking to people? What people? And you two—you and Buskirk's sister—were separated at just about the time of the murder, I understand."

"Why, Zaidee left the dressing room before I did! She went to see if Bill had come in yet!" She was honestly indignant now, but what good did it do?

She had to realize that to be alone at the time of the murder meant opportunity. If she had set it up ahead of time, there had been nothing to prevent her slipping out after Zaidee had left and pushing the stage weight off the ladder.

"Lieutenant, exactly what time was it done? Forty-five minutes is a long time. Can't you pin it down more exactly? Maybe then people will be able to be more accurate for you."

"Your point is well taken," he said judicially. "Of course, we can't be exact, but a couple of factors help us a little. The body was found at 11:45. That's accurate to within a couple of minutes. Took the doc another twenty to arrive because of that damned football game traffic.

"McCord and one of the other stagehands insist that the hand and wrist were turning cold when they felt him for a pulse at 11:45. Now, that area of the backstage, so I'm told, is notoriously chilly. Also, the janitor turned off the central heat promptly at 11:00, figuring the hands would get through with what they had to do before the building cooled down too much."

He looked for a minute through the disorderly pile of notes in front of him. "That means that Schring's death should be placed as soon after the 11:00 finish as possible. From the other end, there's one bit of evidence that's solid: two or three of the players saw him in the bar across the street. So if he dashed over there as soon as the bows were over and only stayed for a quickie, he could have been back here and waiting at the blue dressing room by, say, 11:15."

Nella said, "Don't you have to allow time for him to get impatient and walk over to the lighted area?"

"Yes, but that needn't have taken over five minutes. When you're waiting for someone, especially in the dark, time stretches out."

Earnestly, Nella leaned forward again. "Lieutenant, I'm new in the orchestra this season. I didn't even know Milton Schring very well. Why in the world would I want to kill him?"

"It's my understanding, Miss Payne, that Mr. Schring was pretty much a tyrant within his section. If you had rejected his attentions, maybe he'd have been angry enough to have made your life miserable as a member of this orchestra. Isn't that possible? This job means a lot to you, doesn't it?"

A lot! It was everything. It was proving to her mother and dad that their years of sacrifice for private lessons, and later the conservatory, had all been worth the effort. It was prestige and security, and the blessed opportunity and challenge of playing great music every day. Nella had a painful lump in her throat that threatened to prevent her from answering.

"Yes," she said very quietly, and then, "but Milton Schring wasn't like that. Nothing outside influenced his musical judgment. If I played badly, he'd jump all over me for that. If I played well, he let me know I had. When we were rehearsing or playing a concert, he wasn't interested in any aspect of me except that I played in his section."

When Ross said that was all he wanted to ask, Nella said, "Isn't there a chance of your finding fingerprints on that stage weight, Lieutenant?"

"There was nothing. My men have been over it very carefully, Miss Payne. Too easy to avoid, you see. The murderer didn't even need to wear gloves—just a handkerchief in the hand would have been protection enough."

He and Lyle stood up, and in another minute she was outside. There was Ralph, looking anxious, with Zaidee close behind.

"Are you okay? Was it all right? Zaidee told me . . ."

"Oh, Nella, dammit, I had to tell them about that twenty minutes or so before we met in the dressing room! I didn't want to mention it to you before your interview and make you nervous. But I knew you'd be able to explain it, so . . ."

Nella smiled. "Guess we're even then, Zee. *I* told him about the time you went out to look for Bill."

"What? Oh, that's all right. I'd forgotten. But where did you go right after the concert? I didn't say so to Ross, but I did look around for you backstage. Did you go out or something?"

Nella glanced at Ralph's large bulk. He looked so anxious. Why upset him any more? She took his arm. "I went in rather than out. To meet Trevelyn, courtesy of Oscar Manning. Tell you the details later. Let's get some lunch, shall we?"

Bilbo Jones stood at the row of coat hooks close to the stage door. His hand was in the pocket of his blue sweater, a shabby but comfortable-looking item which hung from the hook numbered "four."

"Forget something, Bilbo?" Ralph asked casually as they neared him.

"No, I'm just fixing it so I won't. Putting my mouthpiece in my pocket so I can't forget to take it home. This one's my favorite. I can't stand to play my practice horn after I've been rehearsing down here with this mouthpiece, so I just carry it back and forth."

"Laziness—sheer laziness!" Zaidee scolded with the freedom of old friendship. "You ought to carry your good instrument home every day!"

Bilbo's nice monkey-face lighted with a smile that curved up his mouth at the corners. "Ahhhh, fiddle players! Wait'll you have a couple of rambunctious kids running all over the house. My good trumpet's a hell of a lot safer down here, locked in my locker."

"Just don't ever get as absent-minded as Pete Rollinson," Ralph said. "You know we're stand partners. Did I tell you this before? No? Well, I got home from rehearsal one day a few weeks ago and went to put up my jacket and damned if there wasn't a mouthpiece in the pocket!

"I thought it was mine, at first. It was a damn good one, but of course I could tell the difference when I put it on my horn and tried it. We'd both had our jackets hanging on the backs of our chairs that day, and old Pete had reached for his own pocket and hit mine by mistake.

"Naturally, I brought it back next rehearsal, but our day off happened to come in between, and poor Rollinson was about ready for suicide when I showed up

63

asking which horn player had lost it."

"How could he do a thing like that?" Zaidee asked.

"Easily, when you come to think about it," Ralph said. "All you need is the same kind of garment, and a touch of absent-mindedness—or being in a hurry."

Nella said, "Why didn't you call Pete and check?"

"I tried a few times, but he's never at home since that roommate of his moved out."

Bilie Jean Jones put her hand around the backstage door. "Surprise!" she smiled. "The Buick's finally fixed. Soon as I can get you to the garage, darling, I'm an independent woman again."

"Too damned independent now," grumbled Bilbo.

The others greeted Billie Jean warmly. With both her own boys in school, she worked as a substitute teacher most days of the week, but she had enough free time to keep up friendly relations with nearly all the Symphony musicians. Even newcomers like Nella and Ralph had already sampled the Joneses' hospitality.

"I'm going to miss Milton," Billie Jean said. "The orchestra isn't going to sound the same without him. Was it very bad this morning, with everybody talking about it?"

"Pretty bad," Bilbo said. "Come on, hon, I told the lieutenant that you and I'd help out with the arrangements. We'd better get moving."

As they threaded their way through traffic toward the garage, Billie Jean said, "I saw Evvie this morning."

"Evvie who?"

"Oh, darling, you're not paying attention. Evvie the viola player, of course. Anyway, she stopped me outside and said she wanted to ask me something privately."

"That's funny."

"What is?"

"Nothing, sorry. Go on, what did Evvie ask you?"

"Well, she was so diffident about it, I thought she'd

never get to the point. But what she wanted to know was, had I seen Toby last night?''

''What's she talking about? She was *with* Toby last night! Both of them said they were having a drink across the street.''

''She meant after that. They had a quarrel, I think about that new music you played last night, and left each other in a huff. Now she's worried that Toby might have gone back inside.''

''Well, what if he did? Though I don't think he did. I never saw him, did you? Why is she worried?''

''Well, she's not exactly worried, but it seems that Milton came over there for a quickie after the concert, and somehow managed to put Toby's back up. Evvie's so vague about things like that, but I think she meant he was flirting with her, in a casual sort of way.''

Bilbo mused, ''Now I see what Toby was questioning me about. Poor old duffer kept it so obscure I never even guessed what he wanted. But basically he was asking me the same thing in reverse.''

''You mean he thought Evvie might have gone back to the Hall?''

''That must be it. He was nattering around, asking me to name all the musicians who gathered when the police came. Asking me if I was sure that was all. Whom had I seen in the hall before that? I kept naming off people for him. What a knothead! Why couldn't he just ask me if I'd seen her?''

''I don't know. Toby isn't your all-time great intellect, but surely he doesn't think that Evvie, in a fit of rage . . . ?''

Bilbo turned his head and looked at her for a long second, till she winced and begged him to watch the road.

''Sorry, hon. But I was just thinking—do you realize how often in the last twenty-four hours or so we've said

'It couldn't possibly be' about one of our friends?''

"Yes, I know exactly what you mean. Sooner or later, we're going to have to admit it could be, and is, one of our friends. At least, I guess we will."

"Maybe not. It may turn out to be an outsider, someone who's cased the Hall thoroughly and used it just to throw suspicion on the musicians instead of himself." He sounded doubtful, remembering his own words to Lieutenant Ross about how much an outsider would have to know.

Billie Jean shuddered. "I don't see how you can make music together, knowing that somebody in the orchestra may have killed Milton."

"We're professionals, remember. Which is not to say you can't tell the difference in our playing. You sure as hell can. That rehearsal this morning was lousy. When John gets back and finds us totally demoralized like this, he's going to go right through the roof. It's a hell of a mess, and nothing's going to make it better until the case is solved."

"*If* it's solved," Billie Jean put in doubtfully. "Some cases never are . . . Bilbo?"

"What, hon?"

"Let's not tell anybody that Toby and Evvie were asking about each other."

"Hon, I don't like withholding anything from the police. It's a bad principle. And Ross told me today he'd forget anything we ever told him if it turned out to have nothing to do with the murder. I believe him. He seems like a straight guy."

"Oh, I agree, when it's anything important. But this is just a silly business between the two of them. You know how they're always quarrelling and making up. It doesn't mean a thing."

"Well, okay for now. As long as it doesn't seem to

add up to anything. And if I change my mind on telling it, I'll tell you first."

"Fair enough."

CHAPTER VII

Lieutenant Ross was leaning back in Robert Lyle's padded desk chair, a hand over tired, momentarily closed eyes. Buskirk knocked and then entered, carrying two large white delicatessen sacks. "Time for lunch?" he said, making it a question.

"Just in time to save a life, my boy," Ross answered. "Who'd you order for?"

"You, me, and Able," Buskirk said. "I thought you might like to mull over the gleanings so far, while we eat."

He set out Poor Boys, napkins, coffee, and fruit pies on the glass-topped table. Stepping to the door, he bellowed for Sergeant Able, who came on the run.

"Just talking with that McCord guy," Able said as he pulled a chair to the desk. "He was discreetly offering his services—for a reasonable fee, you understand—to spy on the orchestra personnel for us."

"Offer him nothing," Ross said dourly. "Our problem with that one will be to keep him out. Be in here every other hour, ratting on somebody."

"What have you got so far, Lieutenant?" Able wanted to know.

"Well, let's see: for a start, there are ninety-eight musicians in this orchestra. That makes ninety-seven people who worked with Schring, observed Schring, and most of whom disapproved of Schring, as far as his treatment of his wife was concerned. They all seem to believe he cheated on her constantly, so it's probably true."

"Current girl friend?"

"Now, it's a funny thing, but nobody seems to know. They all say they wouldn't mind telling; they just don't know. The consensus is he was between affairs."

"Well," Buskirk said, "I suppose that does happen once in a while."

"Right. But it cuts down severely on strong motives. No girl friend, no jilted flame. Also, no big cause for the wife to get angry right now; in fact, less cause for her to kill him than usual."

Able said, "You'll talk to her though?"

Ross looked at his watch. "She's due in here in approximately twenty minutes."

"Now, among the orchestra suspects," Buskirk said, "you've talked to Freed, the guy who tried to get Schring's job. What did you think of him?"

"Same thing you thought," Ross grinned. "Definitely feeling guilty about something. Definitely holding back on why he was in the hall that late. But, you know, if he'd been clever enough to play this murder in advance—and it was a planned thing—surely he'd have been prepared to put on a better act afterwards?"

"I thought that, too," Able said, pleased. "Why would he be in such a state of shock if he'd known what was going to happen?"

"Unless he's double smart," Buskirk said, "and putting on an act."

"Then there's the outside couple," Ross said. "Oldenberg and his wife. Why were they hanging around so late? Don't tell me drinking coffee with that Williams dame is Oldenberg's idea of a good time. That means he was just filling in time, waiting for his wife. So the real question is, what was *she* hanging around backstage so long for?"

"Just visiting, she said," Able answered. "Funny

that she can't remember exactly who she talked to, though; she was pretty vague about that."

Buskirk said, "You've got to remember she's not the law-abiding, conscientious type, itching to help the forces of law and order. She's pretty flighty, and always has been. Not a snob at all, so Zaidee tells me, but she just can't be bothered with remembering things."

"Hmm . . . maybe." Ross began to make marks on the half-full note pad in front of him. "What was your impression of Mr. Robert Z. Lyle?"

"Cold fish," Able began, and hesitated. Ross nodded him on. "Can't imagine him stooping to care enough about a mere clarinet player to murder him. I know, he was ready to help Manning kick Schring out of the orchestra, but it was Manning's project to begin with."

"I still wonder," Ross said thoughtfully, "just who runs this orchestra. You ask three people, you get three different answers. Jones likes to think the musicians have a big say in what happens, but that could be more wishful thinking than reality.

"When you watch Lyle and Manning talking together from a distance, you almost get the impression that Manning is laying down the law and Lyle is taking it, but when you get up close, it turns out that Manning is all but licking his boots."

Buskirk said, "Well, I only know what Zee tells me. The way she sees it, this contract the musicians have now is the best one they've ever had, but not as good as it should be. She says it all harks back to the middle ages, when the artist would have to have a wealthy patron to support him, and he'd live like a beggar on what the rich guy decided to give him. A small exclusive bunch of rich people here in town make up the core of the Symphony League. Zee says they love to mention 'our orchestra' and 'our musicians,' and what they *don't* want is to see money from industry getting into the act.

"That's why there's always a Symphony deficit. They won't go out and solicit donations and endowments, even though these huge companies would be delighted to give for a tax writeoff. Why? They might have to let all those non-aristocrat company presidents into some of their little private clubs."

"You astonish me, Bill," murmured Ross. "Didn't know you could build up a head of steam like that about the Symphony."

Buskirk laughed. "Guess I didn't know it, either," he said. "Let me get back to your question—I was coming around to answering it. Who runs the orchestra: on a daily basis, I'd have to say it's Manning, just because he's always there, seeing what's happening. But on any large issue, he has to have approval from at least Lyle, and probably the whole League Board of Directors."

"All of which brings us to the executive secretary. Quite a powerful man in local music circles apart from the Symphony, so I've been told, and one who prefers to work in the dark—at least figuratively. I picture him pulling strings, getting people hired and fired, without their ever knowing. What do you think of him as a potential killer?" Ross asked.

"Fits like a glove," growled Buskirk. "I can just see that little twerp, sneaking along to the ladder and setting up that weight. His kind of thing, exactly."

"That was my first impression, too," Ross said, rubbing his cheek, "but not my second. Remember: he's clever enough to control the choicest work in this town, and that means controlling the finest musicians this city contains. He can't be a fool. He's survived too long.

"But setting up that weight was a fool kind of stunt. How could he, or anybody, be sure who'd get hit with it? How hard it would hit? Whether the blow would be fatal or not? It was sloppy, boys, sloppy. I can't see a really smart man doing it."

"But suppose," Able said, "he didn't care that much. I mean, suppose he said something to himself like, 'Maybe this'll kill Schring. If so, that's good. If it doesn't, it'll give him a headache, and I'll kill him some other time.' In other words, he wanted him dead, but there was no special deadline."

Ross shook his head doubtfully and went back to his list.

"We haven't touched on the females in the orchestra," he said. "Bill, do you want me to take you off this case? Be more comfortable letting someone else take over here?"

"No, Lieutenant. I've been meaning to say that to you. Zaidee's all right. The only thing that would bother me is if it would bother her to have me around, being a policeman. To tell you the truth, I think she likes it. Gives her a feeling of power, I guess," he grinned.

"That's all right. Just remember you said that, in case we have to give her the third degree."

"What about that Williams dame? Be a pure pleasure to pin something on that one. Didn't you think she was acting suspiciously last night?"

Sergeant Able added, "Starting to say things, and then not saying them. And claiming she couldn't remember where she was for the biggest part of the time!"

Ross said, "I think our Lottie is the type that always acts suspicious. Oh, it wouldn't surprise me at all to find that the woman was involved, last night, in some discreditable enterprise she didn't want to share with us. It would surprise me, though, to learn that she had anything to do with a cold-blooded murder. If there's one thing that woman isn't, it's cold-blooded."

"That's the truth," said Able. "You're right, it's

hard to picture her planning anything, and carrying it out like that. She's too scatty."

"What about the redhead? The Payne girl. There's the time period she didn't account for very adequately," Ross said.

Buskirk said, "What would her motive be? She's brand-new in the orchestra. She won't get solo chair, now that Schring's dead. She must have known she wouldn't. Freed may be the one chosen, or they may pick an applicant from some orchestra in another city. So what does she gain? And I'll say the same thing for Payton, that horn player who's got a crush on her. He's new, too, and Schring could hardly have meant that much to him."

Able said admiringly, "Now how did you know that this horn player has a crush on Nella Payne?"

"I *am* a detective," Buskirk said drily. "As a matter of fact, my sister had been egging me on to date Nella. I'd been meaning to get around to it, too, but by the time I finally got a free night—" he glanced at Ross "—this Payton was already way ahead of me. Old Zee is just going to have to match-make for me some other time."

"So who's left on our list?" Able asked.

"Freed. The Man With a Motive," Ross said.

"What motive? He wouldn't dare take Schring's chair now, after the hassle about it from before. Be too obvious," Able said.

"On the contrary," Ross said, "I am told there will now be advertising for clarinet players to fill the vacancy. Probably, as Bill said, several from nearby towns will apply. There will be blind auditions. Freed will have the same chance as the rest of them—and everybody will know he had to work for it."

"So maybe he did the crime on spec," Sergeant Able said, "if he likes his own playing that much."

A short, middle-aged woman appeared in the doorway, giving a token rap on the open door. She said, "Lieutenant Ross?"

All three men rose to meet Millie Schring. Buskirk began gathering up his things and quietly left the room. Able settled himself quietly on the sofa, his shorthand notebook open on his lap.

Millie Schring's eyes were misty, but she had regained her composure. "I appreciate your seeing me at lunch time, Lieutenant," she said. "It would be so difficult, just now, to have to greet all Milton's old friends."

She didn't seem like a woman who would ever find it difficult to face people. There was solid assurance in her non-nonsense short gray hair that framed her face; her plain but well-shaped nose and mouth; her soft blue dress and navy-and-white accessories.

"As I said on the phone, Mrs. Schring, I'd have been glad to have come to you," Ross said. "We appreciate you coming down like this, but it seems to me it was too much of an imposition on you."

"I believe in doing what is right," Millie Schring said. "When I tell you what I think—or rather, what I suspect—you may agree that it was urgent for you to know this information right away.

"Milton was an unfaithful man, Lieutenant. I suppose you have already been told about it. I learned that fact the first year we were married, twenty-two years ago," she said. "I had gotten used to it. You'd be surprised, perhaps, at some of the things a woman can get used to. At first I stuck to him because I loved him very much. I'd like to say that was my only reason the whole twenty-two years, but that wouldn't be true. After a while, when you live with a man who's always finding someone he likes better, you give up on that aspect of life.

"The girls were growing up, and I will say he was very fond of them, and very careful to keep any hint of scandal away from them. I couldn't have stayed with him otherwise.

"After a while, we moved into a different arrangement, without ever discussing it openly. I got a part-time job in a flower shop. Milton chased his women and I filled up my spare time with civic work. He was always a good provider, had a great many private students, and never seemed to tire. He's left me with a very comfortable income from a large term life insurance policy. I plan to keep on working, too.

"So I can look upon this terrible thing with more objectivity than you might believe, Lieutenant. But I do still care—more than I realized—and I mean to see that the murderer is punished. She mustn't get away with this."

"She!"

"Oh yes, she. The pity is, I don't know which she. But that's what I've come to tell you, Lieutenant. It had to be one of his women. I know his pattern, you see. Two months for a short romance. Five or six for a really big one. But always, always he got tired of the woman first. He needed to be the rejecting one, as much as he needed the women. Don't ask me why! He didn't grow like that as we went along; he was like that the first day I ever set eyes on him.

"What you need is to find out what woman he started an affair with last summer, say, June or July. I knew it had ended five or six weeks ago. I can always tell when that happens. I'm sorry now that I haven't kept better in touch with his orchestra friends. Then I'd know which woman it was, probably. But I didn't care to be pitied."

With a rather heroic lunge, Ross took charge of the conversation. "Mrs. Schring, I can't tell you how much we appreciate your frankness. It makes my job so much easier. And speaking of my job, there is the routine aspect of it. I'm sure you understand that we also need a formal statement from you as to your whereabouts last night. For the record.''

She shook her head, a little confused. "But what has that to do with . . . ? Oh, of course, you have a set procedure, don't you? Of course, it seems so strange. Imagine anyone thinking I might hurt Milton. There there was a time . . .''

When she drifted into silence, staring straight ahead at something far away, Sergeant Able stepped forward. "Mrs. Schring. Sergeant Able. Could you tell me, please, where you were last night between eleven and twelve o'clock?''

"Why, I was in Ohio. Your department called me there. I came in on Flight 797, Pan American, this morning. Both our daughters are away in college but they're coming home today, of course. Some of the neighbors are meeting them at the airport for me. But I was out of state last night.''

"Did anyone else besides our department get in touch with you last night? A friend; someone from the Symphony?''

"No, I heard nothing until . . . they phoned me from here. I was alone at my cousin's home at the time.''

"That's all we need right now, thank you,'' Ross said gently.

She gathered up her purse and looked around blankly for a moment for gloves she had never taken off. "If you need me for anything else, call me. I won't mind. We mustn't let her get away with this!''

The desk phone buzzed as Millie Schring walked out. Able answered, "Sergeant Able. Yes, he's right here. Just one minute,'' and handed over to Ross.

"This is Helene Lyle, Lieutenant. I'm calling for Mrs. Smallwood. Mrs. *Verna* Smallwood . . . ?''

Ross hunted around his mind for the connection. The name was familiar, but it refused to click. Finally he said, "Just a minute, please," and asked Buskirk, "who's Verna Smallwood?"

Buskirk said softly, "Rich old widow. Symphony League."

"Yes, Mrs. Lyle. Yes, I'll be happy to speak to her . . . Mrs. Smallwood. How do you do? Elvin Ross, here. Well, it's rather difficult to say, this early, just how well the investigation's going. We're still getting statements from people."

The crackly little voice said, "That's why I'm calling, Lieutenant. There's something about one of the stage-hands I thought I ought to tell you."

"What's that, ma'am?"

"It's Regal McCord I'm talking about. The stringy one, you know, with the yellowish hair? He used to be one of our household staff."

"Oh, really? Did you have any problems?"

"Well, yes. That's why he's not our chauffeur any more. I found him to be quite a troublemaker, first of all. The man seems to like telling one person stories about another, just to see the fur fly. I didn't understand what was happening for quite a while, in fact until he had a regular feud going between the cook and two of the maids.

"I probably wouldn't have fired him just for that. At least, I called him in and tried to change him by a good talking-to. He tried to be high-handed with me at first and bluff it out, but I don't bluff very easily."

Something in the quavery old voice made Ross think she was right. Somehow, Verna Smallwood didn't sound like the type you could fool for very long.

She went on, "Then he tried crawling. Disgusting. I told him to straighten up and be a man if he wanted to keep working for me. He said he did want to, but events proved otherwise."

"What happened?"

"What happened next was a forged check. One I had given him for car expenses. The amount was filled out, but not the payee. I must admit, my handwriting is deteriorating somewhat," she sighed. "I believe it was quite easy for him to slip a '1' in front of my '2,' and change the written two into twelve."

"Do you mean from 'two hundred' to 'twelve hundred,' Mrs. Smallwood?"

"Exactly, Lieutenant. I have no idea what went through the man's mind. Perhaps he thought, since we live so comfortably, we would be careless enough not to notice." Her voice became grim. "People who are well off usually are not at all careless with money, Lieutenant. I may say, that comes close to a contradiction in terms."

Ross chuckled along with her. "That's been my own experience, Ma'am. Now may I ask what you did about the check?"

"I'm a widow, Lieutenant. I have to run my own affairs, except I do have my secretary, Annie. She's a flighty young thing, and not much help in situations like this. I keep her because she types well and knows how to be nice to people. And she needs the money.

"Anyway, I called Regal in when Annie could be there for moral support. I confronted him with the check, and told him my banker had advised me to prosecute—which he had. I told him he would have to leave my employ at once; he could have a month's salary, but there could be no notice and no recommendation."

"But you didn't prosecute? File charges, I mean?"

"No. He had only spent three hundred of the money, and he restored the rest. I couldn't bring myself to file charges. He was such a pitiful object. All alone in the world, apparently, and he pleaded so. I finally told him just to get out as fast as he could."

"And the stagehand job?"

"It's only partly my fault that he's there. He had an uncle who was a stagehand and who, I believe, pulled some strings for him. Regal called me about a month after he'd left our house, and begged me to make just one phone call to put in a good word for him with Robert Lyle. Not that Robert has the hiring and firing of the hands, but he has some kind of approval rights.

"It seemed rather a small favor to ask, and I was sorry for the wretched man—so I did it." She drew a long breath as if she were glad to have the story told.

"Now, I've been making notes on all this, Mrs. Smallwood," Ross said, "and to summarize a bit: I understand that you felt I should know McCord is not a very trustworthy character."

"Yes, I suppose that covers it. I was uneasy, especially since he was the one who discovered poor Mr. Schring's body. I hated to think of you being in the position of relying on his word for anything."

"I appreciate your calling, Ma'am. Do I remember correctly that you were there yourself that night?"

"That's true, Lieutenant. And I was backstage after the concert, as well. Would you like me to come down and give you a statement?"

Ross pictured the tiny little bag of bones that Verna Smallwood had become. In the newspaper she always looked a foot shorter than everyone around her. A potent little pygmy surrounded by giants. "No, thanks," he said gravely. "Not at the present, anyway."

"Please don't hesitate to phone me if I can help you that way, or any way," she insisted. "My time is usually filled, but I can always make room to help your investigation. This violence in our orchestra is dreadful. I shan't be happy until it is solved."

Ross thanked her again and hung up. He treated Able and Buskirk to a brief review of her end of the conversation.

"What difference does it make?" said Able.

"None, that I know of," Ross said. "But I'd rather know he's unreliable now than later—just in case something else does come up."

CHAPTER VIII

If you ignored the aggressively knotty pine paneling, the barbecue place three blocks from the concert hall was an excellent place for lunch. Settled into one-armed chairs with steaming sandwiches of succulent beef slices, they talked over the murder again.

"Schring was a stinker, a gifted stinker," Ralph summarized. "But I just can't see why anybody would be angry enough to murder him. For example, Freed. He's no fool. He knows after that audition that he didn't deserve the solo chair. Did you see how nervous he was today, playing it?"

"He was willing to take it when Manning and Lyle were trying to steal it for him," Nella retorted.

"All right, but taking it on a platter's a lot different from killing to get it," Ralph said. "Can you picture Freed dropping that weight on Schring?"

"Freed isn't the violent type," Nella agreed absently. She was experiencing that meanest of small frustrations, a blocked idea. Ever since they had left the hall, some thought had been trying to ring a bell in the back of her mind. What *was* it?

Zaidee wasn't following the conversation; she was too annoyed. "'Did you hear what that little jackass announced during the break?" she demanded. They hadn't heard Manning's announcement. He'd only called for the attention of the second violins.

"We're going to have an hour's section rehearsal tomorrow afternoon . . . just the second violins. Because *somebody* isn't cutting the part!"

81

Nella and Ralph clucked in accord with her indignation. The section rehearsal would be unpaid, technically an illegal service. It wasn't a big enough issue to fight through the union, but it was a type of petty chiseling of extra time and services at which Manning was expert. The ironic thing was, everybody knew who wouldn't be playing the part—who always had difficulty with a first reading of a part.

There were two weak, inexperienced players at the back of the section, and there was Lottie Williams, who could never be bothered to take the music home and "woodshed" the difficult passages. Eventually, she would get the notes right. Probably the weak players would, too, or they would fake their way through the concert. In the meantime, the whole section of second violins had to stay and suffer.

Zaidee went on, "The damned thing is, he knows *I* won't complain. He always calls me for the ballet and the auto shows, and I need the extra money."

There it was again. Manning's stranglehold on some of the best jobbing dates in town kept musicians from forcing a showdown with him through the union.

"Well, anyway, the morning session won't be but an hour," Ralph reminded them. "Bilbo set the funeral for 10:30 so everybody who wanted to go could get there, and get back for the afternoon half."

"Let's go together, shall we? Bill's picking me up at the Hall, and there's plenty of room for you and Nella. Then your cars will be here already."

"Fine with me," Nella said as Ralph nodded acceptance. "Then I'll wait for you after the section rehearsal, Zee, and take you home with me for supper. All right?"

Remarkable how a murder "in the family" made you cling to your friends, Nella thought. The three of them sat there, all feeling relieved at plans not to be alone the next day.

"By the way, Nell, you said you'd explain later about that time when Zaidee was waiting for you in the dressing room." Ralph tried to keep the possessive note out of his voice that he felt was creeping in. Already he was feeling a great deal more proprietary toward Nella than he considered it wise to show. Better wait until he knew for sure how she felt about him.

"Oh, that." Her voice went a little higher as she tried for just the right, light tone. "Just a couple of trivial things, really. Manning insisted that I come along and have a cup of coffee with Trevelyn. It was embarrassing. I've never been to England, and didn't know a thing to talk about . . . and then Manning came along after me when I excused myself and left. He . . . he wanted a date." She glanced at Ralph quickly, and then away.

Surely he'd know she had refused Manning. Not just because of Manning's long-suffering, faithful wife, but because she certainly had better taste than that!

But she'd better not be so confident that Ralph was all that interested in her private life. Better wait till she knew for sure how he felt about her.

"Do I detect a passionate interlude?" demanded Zaidee. "What did he do, Nell, make a pass at you?"

"Something like that."

"Be flattered, hon. Oh, not because of the pass! Manning makes a pass at every new woman who comes along. But because he made it a clinch instead of a pinch. To Manning's way of thinking, there are just two types of females around—the clinchers and the pinchers. I've always considered it more socially desirable to be thought of as a clincher."

Ralph glowered at the tablecloth, saying nothing, but Nella laughed, grateful that Zaidee had managed to lighten the moment.

She said, "Well, it proves one thing, doesn't it? Since Manning was occupying himself with me, he couldn't also be setting up the booby trap for Milton."

Ralph said, "What's wrong with before he met you or afterward? That thing could have been set up any time at all, don't forget."

They separated at the parking lot. Nella had the feeling that she forgot something but she couldn't quite place what it was. Half a day off! Usually, Wednesdays were totally free, but in shuffling schedules for the guest conductor they'd gotten behind in services, and had had to make up with the morning's work.

Nella scooted her little economy car through light noonday traffic to the pleasant old suburb where she had an apartment. It was shabby-respectable, like the one-time mansion it was in. Its great charm for Nella was in the outside stairs which she used most of the time. They led to a small landing where she had several planter boxes started, and where her kitchen door opened.

Nella stopped for groceries at the local store. She trundled her paper sacks up the stairs in three trips. Then it was time for the last trip, the Wednesday treat: the library.

The walk was just long enough to be good exercise. Her only problem was disciplining herself to keep down the number of books she had to carry back and forth. I'm going to be an awful old tabby before I'm thirty-five, she told herself. Here I am, twenty-five, and I even have a set routine for visiting the library! She grinned to herself, and to the mildly surprised librarian, as she passed the desk. In a life as irregular as a musician's, having a few comfortable routines makes a delightful change.

First stop was the mystery section. Long ago she had exhausted the library's supply of Tey, Marsh and

Christie. Now she had to pick and sample, testing carefully for flavor and background. English settings appealed to her most; with a small community background, like a village or an institution.

On to biographies, and then to the history section. Nella stopped herself at six books, though eight were allowed to be checked out at one time. She had more than enough material to last two weeks, in case there wasn't time to come back next Wednesday.

She had to set things down on the porch landing to unlock the kitchen door, fumbling with haste as the telephone began ringing inside. How nice if it was Ralph! But the phone stopped just when she raced into the bedroom and snatched it up.

After she'd put everything away and decided on a hamburger dinner, Nella gave up listening for the phone and began shampooing her hair in the kitchen sink. Then, of course, the phone rang again. Through a wad of towel and the mild popping of soapsuds, she heard Lottie Williams's voice. It was unconvincingly light and nonchalant.

"My, my! How'd I get so lucky as to catch our glamour girl at home? Or am I interrupting something? Just say the word if you have company."

"No, Lottie, I'm by myself. Just washing my hair, as a matter of fact."

Lottie considered that she had spent enough time on preliminaries. "Listen, Nella, I've been thinking about this Schring thing."

Schring thing, ring a ding, ching ring, ran wickedly through Nella's mind. Hideous little coincidence of rhyme!

"Thinking what about it, Lottie?"

Lottie's voice lowered to a portentous hiss. "*I know who pushed that weight off the ladder!*"

As so often happened with Lottie, Nella didn't know

whether to laugh, groan, or snarl with disgust. It never crossed her mind to take the words seriously. Still, she played it straight; it was easier. "Lottie, if you know who did it, you should be calling the police, not me."

"The police! That *boor*! Can't you imagine his stupid reaction? I didn't say I could prove it. I just said, I know who did it. I suppose you wouldn't care to know who it was?"

There was only one shortcut that worked with Lottie; move directly to the point she was going to make eventually. "Who was it, Lottie?"

"Can't you guess? Think, Nella! Who's going to benefit from Schring's death?"

"His widow, I should think—oh! You mean musically."

"Exactly. Who else but Freed? Wasn't he trying to chisel his way into solo chair before? And didn't he wind up playing it, finally, today?"

"Oh, but now there'll be auditions. You know that! People from orchestras all around will put in their bids, too, I'm sure. Why wouldn't they? So Freed could get it—he's really good, I think—but it's no cut and dried cinch."

Lottie sidetracked herself momentarily. "Sure you wouldn't like it yourself, hon?"

"Of course not! I don't have any delusions of being ready for principal, after only three months in the orchestra. I'm just saying that if Freed does get it, it'll be because he earned it."

"So suppose he has that much self-confidence? Just naturally assumes that with Schring out of the way, he's in? He's got a mighty cool exterior, but let me tell you, under the surface is one enormous ego."

"Do you really believe that? He always struck me as being so shy."

"Try conceited instead. Too full of himself to bother

making friends with us peasants.''

Nella began to recognize the drift. A person only needed to walk past Lottie absentmindedly, once, to be condemned in this manner. Either that, or perhaps Freed at some time had failed to mask his contempt for Lottie's goings-on.

''Now, really, Lottie, I do think it's dangerous for us to start accusing each other without any evidence. How do you know some of the others aren't talking about one of us on the phone right now, saying you or I did it?''

''Who said I didn't have any evidence? All I said was, I couldn't *prove* Freed did it. Not yet, that is. Wait and see.''

''Lottie, listen, if you really do know something, you *must* tell Lieutenant Ross. Don't you see that it would be too dangerous not to?''

''Only if the wrong person knows what I know. And you're the only one I'm telling,'' Lottie added.

That'll be a first, Nella thought grimly. Lottie telling only one person a piece of gossip like this! Suddenly she was very tired of the argument. Talking with Lottie always felt like pushing against a stone wall. Little trails of soapy water were beginning to seep under the towel and down her neck.

''Lottie, my hair's dripping. Thanks for calling, but I really have to get back to my shampoo.''

Starting again with the hot water, she wondered if she had discounted Lottie's suspicions too much. Could she really know something? So many times Lottie's big mysteries dissolved into little, attention-getting devices. Was this time any different?

She decided to soothe both mind and conscience by devoting the rest of the evening to practice. As soon as she had cleaned up the kitchen after her meal, she gathered up her horns, set her desk chair before the dresser, propped an exercise book upright in a convenient drawer, and began.

Playing the third, or "doubling" clarinet chair, she was responsible to play bass clarinet, E-flat or B-flat clarinet as the literature demanded. There was even an occasional saxophone part. She had to avoid the persistent danger of getting rusty.

Just when she was thinking of quitting in favor of the ten o'clock news, the phone rang. She jumped for it. Ralph? No. A strange voice, in fact a peculiar sounding one. She didn't understand a word it said, the first time.

"What was that? I couldn't understand you. Are you sure you have the right number?" she asked. Now the voice changed completely. She knew it was disguised, but this time it spoke clearly. When it finished, Nella heard the click, followed by a dial tone.

"See you later," the voice had said. "Remember? 'See you later.' " That was all.

She slammed down the receiver, disgusted. Now, what had that stupidity been about? Was it a quote? From whom? Was it supposed to scare her? Ever since the murder—only last night, incredibly—people seemed not to be able to talk straight and say what they meant. Well, she wasn't going to be intimidated. Why should she be? The killing, terrible as it was, had absolutely nothing to do with her. She would keep it that way.

Then she remembered, with a glance at her watch, that she still had Milton's instrument. Surely ten o'clock wasn't too late to call? She'd have to go to rehearsal too early to call tomorrow. After a couple of rings, a woman's voice answered, "Schring residence."

"This is Nella Payne. Is this Millie?"

"No, this is her mother. Millie is getting ready for bed. May I take a message, please?"

"Oh, of course. I'm sorry to call so late, but I really haven't had a chance till now. I only wanted to let her

88

know I have Milton's clarinet. I took it home with me last night, and will get it to her as soon as I can." The woman took her name and jotted down the message. Coolly she thanked Nella for calling and hung up.

The phone rang again almost immediately. Expecting the anonymous voice once more, Nella snatched it up and snapped, "Hello!"

"Hello, beautiful," said Ralph's voice. "Do you always sound cordial like that at night, or did I wake you up?"

"Oh . . . Ralph!" Tears came into her eyes, but she gave a big swallow and prevented them from taking her by the throat. "It's so good to hear a human voice . . ."

"Who else has been calling you, orangutans?"

"Maybe. Anyway, somebody anonymous. No, not obscene. He may be trying to be funny. 'See you later' was all he said. Then he repeated it. He said, 'Remember? See you later' like that. That's all there was to it. Tell me I'm making a mountain out of a molehill."

"Very likely you are. Anyway, it's a possibility we should definitely keep in mind. But no, I don't think you're being silly at all. It doesn't really matter what an anonymous caller *says* on the phone. It's his intention to disturb you or frighten you that is upsetting."

"But why such a dumb choice of phrase? 'See you later!' People say that to each other every time they turn around. I say it myself all the time."

Ralph said thoughtfully, "I know. I heard someone say it to you the other night. I guess it stuck in my mind because *I* was going to see you later. Tuesday night. Last night, in fact."

"Who said it to me?"

"Milton Schring."

"But I don't—oh, yes, I do remember. Zaidee asked me what he meant by it."

"What did he mean by it?"

"I don't *know*." Nella began to wonder, desperately, how unconvincing this sounded. "It was just before the concert, see, so I told Zee he must mean the overture we were going to play. I didn't have any plan to see him after the concert."

"Of course you didn't," Ralph said mildly. "But I am wondering, Nella, if he thought you did."

"How could he? There was nothing I said to him that could be interpreted that way. Nothing."

"No—but how about that note? Why couldn't Milton have thought it was from you, and that you were getting interested in him?"

"But what a stupid way to put it . . . 'if you're serious.' I'd never have worded it that way, even if I had really wanted a romance with him."

"Of course not. But did he know you well enough to know you wouldn't? Struck me that for a Don Juan type, Milton really understood very little about women."

"I see. Yes, of course you're right. Milton wouldn't know anything about what I might say or write, and he wouldn't particularly care."

"That's enough of that," Ralph said. "I just felt an impulse to phone you, see how you were getting along."

"You have good impulses," Nella said. "I feel a lot better after talking to you. Things seem to be back in perspective now."

"Always happy to oblige, ma'am," he said lightly. "Now, if that phone call really worried you, why don't you take the thing off the hook for the rest of the night?"

"I don't think I'll do that," Nella said. "As it happens, I have a talent you don't know about. I can whistle with two fingers in my mouth, fit to split your eardrums. Just let him call me again. I'll be ready for him this time!"

Ralph chuckled dubiously. "Why, you little rascal! Well, have fun. See you in the morning."

CHAPTER IX

Thursday usually was a double rehearsal day, but this time the morning session would be just an hour because of the funeral. Ross showed up as the tuneup began. So did Robert Z. Lyle. He met Ross at the door and waved him into the plush little office that was reserved for his occasional use backstage.

"Shut the door, will you?" Lyle said, in a tone accustomed to being obeyed. At least, thought Ross dryly, he hadn't added, "my good fellow."

Very much the Chairman of the Board, Lyle waved him into a leather chair and began. "I thought you had better know, Mr. Ross, that the League is quite disturbed by this . . . matter. Perhaps I need not remind you that a good number of the most important civic leaders in the city are Symphony League members.

"We have developed a theory that Mr. Schring's death might have been a tragic, a most regrettable, accident. Someone may have brushed by that weighted rope and accidentally dislodged it. Perhaps it was tucked up onto the ladder like that, in the first place, to get it out of people's way.

"Now, we were in touch yesterday afternoon and this morning with the mayor and the Chief of Police. What we are interested in, Mr. Ross, are speedy results— speedy results and no public furor." He leaned his thickening but still athletic body back in the chair and nodded the silver mane at Ross.

Ross had fished out a writing pad and ballpoint pen during the little lecture. He nodded back energetically.

"That makes two of us, Mr. Lyle. Let's start with a few questions."

It was not the subservient response Lyle had expected. "Questions? Of *me*? Really! This is just the time-wasting sort of thing I've been warning the chief about! What can I possibly tell you that will help your investigation?"

"For openers, where exactly you were from the end of the concert until the body was discovered," said Ross calmly.

Lyle was not the type that went red with indignation. He went white, even to his fist that unconsciously clenched itself on the desk as he leaned forward to speak in a low, intense voice.

"Mr. Ross. It seems you do not appreciate my position here. I am not one of the musicians." It sounded as if he had said, "hired hands." "I direct—it might be more realistic to say, I control—the destinies of this orchestra. I am not here to be questioned."

Ross also leaned forward. He spoke just as intensely. "Mr. Lyle. I think *you* do not appreciate your position here in respect to this investigation—or mine.

"To me, you are just one more human being on the scene, as capable of doing violence as any other. Violence has been done here, make no mistake about that. McCord and all the other hands swear that that stage weight hadn't been out of the box it belonged in for the past three months. On top of that, there's the note that was found in Schring's pocket.

"Please dismiss any other considerations from your mind. This is murder all right, and there is no possibility that it can be made to look like an accident. It's my job first of all to find out who was physically in a position to do it. After I narrow down the field, I can start looking at individual motives and personalities.

"As to controlling destinies, please don't labor under

the delusion that you can control mine. I'm damn good at my job, and the chief and the mayor both know it. If you have the power to pressure them into firing me—which I doubt—I won't worry about it. I'm good enough at what I do to work anywhere."

A thunderous silence fell. Ross clicked his pen and sat back in a comfortable writing position. "Now, let's start with the applause after the last number. Where were you then?"

"Backstage." Lyle seemed to have recovered his poise, but his silver eyebrows shot up as if he were surprised at himself for answering.

"Where, exactly, backstage?"

"At stage right, by the light panel, just behind the curtains. That's on your left, as you look at the stage from the audience," he added grimly. "I shook hands with the maestro when he came off, and waited for him while he took his bows."

"How many bows did he take?"

"Four. He's extremely popular in this country."

"And you waited for him the whole time, and walked off with him. Where?"

"We went into the Mauve Room. It's set aside for visiting conductors and artists, a place where they can be private before a performance. It has its own dressing room and bathroom, and a little sitting room."

"Did anyone else go with you?"

"Manning came on. The personnel manager. With that girl, the red-haired one—clarinetist? And a waiter was there."

"Did you order something?"

"Scotch and water, for Manning and me. The girl wouldn't partake. She seemed pretty gauche. Trevelyn wanted tea."

"Now, thinking of the backstage as a horseshoe, with the light panel at the left end, this Mauve Room is

94

around toward the right end, isn't it? Anyway, past the midpoint? Just about three doors from the blue dressing room that Schring was lying next to?"

Lyle looked as if he meditated balking, but he didn't. "I think . . . there's the Mauve Room, then a ladies' room and a men's room, then the blue dressing room. The . . . body was between the men's room and the dressing room."

"In front of the ladder that's attached to the wall. Yes. And on the other side of the blue room, an outside exit, is that right? Then some more dressing rooms."

"That is correct."

"Now, how long did you wait for your drinks?"

"Seven minutes, possibly ten. Manning took his and darted off. Made some feeble-sounding excuse. I can't imagine what Trevelyn thought of that."

"And how long did you take, drinking your drinks and talking?"

"I have no idea. Really, Mr. Ross—"

Ross sighed. Lyle really had been much more cooperative than he'd expected. Probably he could be soothed along the rest of the way. "Just about finished, Mr. Lyle. Let's see now, figure two minutes per bow, four bows, call it eight to ten minutes. Walk slowly around to the Mauve Room—the conductor must have stopped to talk to a few people?"

"There were a number of interruptions."

"Call it 11:15 when you were in the room and ordering. Say ten minutes for the drinks to come. 11:25. Then you must have relaxed and visited awhile?"

"Trevelyn's driver came for him pretty soon. I stayed there until they came to tell me about the—accident."

Ross let the insinuation pass. "Did you have any other interruptions? Anyone come, or leave the room?"

"Manning was the only one who left, besides the waiter. And the girl, of course."

"Why do you think Manning left?"

Distaste twitched Lyle's silver brows. "Chasing after the girl, I shouldn't wonder. She left right before the drinks came in. He waited long enough to snatch his, and then ran off."

"Why did he bring her in, since she was so self-conscious?"

"Mr. Manning is not above showing off his familiarity with world-renowned conductors to attractive young ladies."

"And you and the conductor did not leave the room at all?"

"No—oh, the maestro stepped into the bathroom for a moment. Neither of us left at all till his driver came."

"Thank you very much, Mr. Lyle." Neither expecting nor receiving a reply, Ross folded back the pages on his pad and rose to leave.

There was a sharp rap, and the door swung inward. The first thing that followed it was a walking cane. It was black and glittered wickedly at the neck about five inches below the crook, where it had a jewelled collar. Lyle sprang to his feet. Already standing, Ross stared in amazement at the tiniest, most wrinkled, shriveled-looking little old lady he had ever seen.

She wore a calf-length, black and white print dress. He supposed it was silk. Pearl drops dangled from her flabby earlobes. Her head was thrust forward on the wrinkled little neck as if the ropes of pearls she wore were dragging her down.

Close behind her was a tall, rather gaunt-looking but very well-dressed lady. Her shoulder length brown hair was perfectly groomed. So were her hands, which were stretched out on either side of the old lady on guard for a stumble.

"Robert!" the tall woman snapped. "Mrs. Smallwood wants to sit down."

Lyle practically tumbled over himself in his haste to oblige. "Of course, my dear. Dear Mrs. Smallwood! How wonderful to see you! It's been so long—we heard you haven't been up to par lately . . . ."

While he talked, he was turning the big leather chair, taking her elbow, urging the old lady toward it. She resisted, warding him off with a glittering, gnarled hand.

"I can't sit in that, Robert. Never get out of it again. Find me a straight chair, please. There, that'll do." She sank gratefully down to rest, but the old back stayed as straight as she could hold it. She leaned forward to rest her prominent chin on the cane and eyed Ross suspiciously.

"Who is this?"

"Why, this is Mr.—ah, Lieutenant Ross. Of the Homicide Division."

Not waiting for an introduction her husband seemed reluctant to make, the tall woman thrust her hand forward to Ross. "I'm Helene Lyle. How do you do?" Her handshake was brief but firm. "Mrs. Smallwood and I came down so that Robert could take us to the funeral. She felt we really ought to go."

"Homicide? I thought it was an accident." The old lady turned accusingly to Lyle.

Lyle said, "Why, Mrs. Smallwood, you see the police have to check out happenings like this. Have to check all the possibilities, you know. We just haven't quite convinced the lieutenant, here, that the whole thing was a terrible accident." He tried for a grin but then decided against it.

The old lady wasn't fooled. "The papers didn't sound like an accident either, Robert. That's one reason I wanted to get here early; wanted to ask you about that. It sounded to me as if someone had planned a booby trap for Milton Schring."

Ross decided to settle the matter. "That's exactly what happened, Mrs. Smallwood. We are investigating everyone who was in the vicinity during the critical time, from right after the concert until the body was found. You'll remember, I asked on the phone about your being here that night."

She nodded her head vigorously as a fit of coughing delayed her answer. "Yes. I've only been to that one concert this year, although my season tickets are for Tuesdays. I had a heart attack, of sorts, last August. Fool of a doctor insisted that I stay flat on my back for three months, and in my house for the next six months. I'm not supposed to be here now, but I don't take orders very well." She smiled with surprising charm.

"My husband was very, very fond of symphonic music, and so am I," she said confidentially to Ross. "We like to look out for our musicians. When this terrible thing happened, I just had to come see what I could do to help you."

Ross was sincerely touched. "Why, ma'am, I don't know exactly . . ." he began.

Bilbo Jones appeared in the doorway. "Hello, darling! Did you come to attend the funeral with Billie and me?" Leaning over the wrinkled cheek, he gave it a friendly peck.

"Thank you, Bilbo, but no. Helene offered Robert's services, so I'm going with them." She patted his hand affectionately.

"Oh, hello, Mrs. Lyle. Nice to see you again." Bilbo turned back to the old lady. "I heard you were going strong and picking up speed, but I didn't know you were quite off the leash yet. Weren't you at the concert last Tuesday?"

"Chewed through the leash, Bilbo. That's what you have to do with those super-cautious doctors nowadays. I'm not even supposed to be out of the house yet."

She asked about Billie Jean and each of the boys, though she got their names and ages mixed up. "They've gotten too old for my parties," she complained. "I never see them any more."

Lyle had had about all the fraternizing with musicians he could take. "Suppose we adjourn to the Mauve Room," he suggested, looking at his watch. "There's a little time before we need to be going. We can have some coffee or tea sent in. I think the lieutenant would like to work in here." He added an anxious postscript to his wife, "If that's all right with you, dear?"

Helene nodded curtly at him. "Come along, then. Ready, Mrs. Smallwood?"

Verna Smallwood's little hand rested in Lieutenant Ross's for an instant. "Remember: I want to help you if I can."

"Thanks, Mrs. Smallwood. I won't forget. It was nice to meet you."

"There goes a lady," said Bilbo under his breath as he and Ross watched her totter away. Both Lyles walked a little behind her, afraid to touch her but alert for slips and wobbles.

"Heard about her all my life," Ross said. "Never thought I'd meet her. Her husband must have died the richest man in the state. It wasn't oil, was it?"

"Banking. And real estate. His family—and hers, too, I think—were Old South originally, and migrated here when the town started growing into a city. Aristocrats from way back, on both sides. They're typical of what's right with the Symphony—and what's wrong with it."

"How do you mean, wrong with it?"

"Well, what you see in the paper is the good side. Giving all that money, working in the fund drives, appealing to all their rich friends to support us. The part you don't read is that they want to keep it all inside their little closed circle. They don't solicit outside contributors, and they don't want them. Did you hear her, just before I came in, say 'our musicians'? That's just the way they think of us."

Ross shook his head. "This case is being very educational for me. I always thought you musicians existed in a permanent state of bliss, on cloud nine."

Bilbo laughed. "Surprise! We like to eat regularly, just like the rest of the world. Say, how old do you think that old lady is?"

"Oh . . ." Ross speculated. "At least eighty. Eighty-five?"

"Would you believe ninety-six? Oh, yes, it's six years now since we had a gala concert for her ninetieth birthday. Just about gave her a heart attack that time, she was so pleased."

"My God! I hope I look that good when I'm ninety-six."

"Hope I'm here to look any way, at that age," said Bilbo soberly.

Stepping out of the office to wait for Billie Jean, Bilbo met Toby Whitemore. He was looking so gloomy that his huge frame seemed bowed down with misery.

"Could I ask you a favor, Bilbo? Do you have any extra room in your car? I was wondering if I could go to the funeral with you," he said.

"Plenty of room," Bilbo said. "We're only take Sample. Be a shame to drive so many cars when there's no need."

"That's good, then," said Toby, not looking as if he meant it. "Evvie hasn't been speaking to me since we played that damned Statiger piece last Tuesday, so I haven't been able to ask her to go with me."

Bilbo chuckled. Evvie and Toby were always finding some excuse for a battle. "Now, how did she manage to blame that on you? You don't pick the program."

"No, but I let her know I liked it. At least, I liked some of it, and said so. The man does have some interesting ideas, and after all, somebody has to be the first to try something new. Why do women have to be so damned conservative?"

"Well, I hate to see you two having a fuss," Bilbo said carefully, "especially when Evvie was so concerned for you the other night."

"So concerned? What other night?"

"Why, Tuesday night. Or at least, she was asking Billie Jean the next day whether you'd come back to the Hall. She was worried, you know, that the police would be harassing you."

"But that's what I was asking you about! About Evvie, I mean. Don't you remember, we split up at the bar across the street—I told you—and I got to thinking later, maybe she went back inside, and was looking upset, you know, and maybe the police would be bothering her."

Bilbo completed the picture for him: "Well, if you thought she had gone inside, and she thought you had gone inside, I suppose really neither of you . . ."

"Bilbo! She's got to care about me, or she wouldn't have been asking Billie Jean. Maybe she was even jealous."

"You've got it, Toby."

"But she won't speak to me! So how can I tell her that I was worried about her, too?" Toby was half laughing at himself, but he was half serious, too. "Say, Bilbo, do you think Billie Jean would . . ."

"Wouldn't be surprised if she would. She's a sucker for star-crossed lovers." He looked at his watch. "We'll have to get a move on, though. I'll go roust out Billie Jean. She must be here by now. I'll give her five minutes to put the message across to Evvie. Where'll you be?"

"By the main exit. That's the safest place to catch

her. Anyway, my car's out there. Thanks a million, Bilbo.'' He fetched Bilbo a slap on the back that propelled him several feet along the hall.

"That's okay, buddy. Can't stand gratitude.'' Bilbo righted himself and hurried away.

CHAPTER X

When the brief morning session ended, most musicians found time for a cup of coffee and a few minutes' chat before going to the funeral home. Nella, going back for her case, passed the row of numbered hooks where the musicians hung their coats and sweaters.

Suddenly the idea she'd been trying to realize came sharply into focus. At the same instant, she saw Ross step out of Lyle's office. She hurried over to catch him.

"Good morning, Miss Payne."

"Oh, Lieutenant Ross, I've just remembered something. Maybe it's nothing, but I thought, perhaps it could have been this way . . ."

As they moved away, Lyle came back around the bend for his forgotten briefcase. He frowned. That was the girl Manning had had in tow Tuesday night. What was she up to?

In a deserted spot near the towering harp case, Nella hurried to explain before the idea got away from her again.

"It's about the hooks, Lieutenant, those numbered hooks on the wall with the blue strip painted behind them. You noticed them? There are twenty-five there, and three more different colored strips of them at different places backstage. Enough for everybody to have one."

"What on earth for—oh! Coats and things."

"Exactly." Nella smiled, pleased to find Ross so easy to talk to today. "Well, we draw for the numbers. You might get blue nineteen, or green four, do you see? But we really stick to our own hooks. It might not sound like much of a problem, but when five men come in at odd times and dump five black overcoats on, say, that piano over there . . . ! So we're particular about it."

Ross said patiently, "Yes, Miss Payne. You mean, each musician has a place to hang his sweater or coat while he's working."

"Yes. And wasn't that note that Schring had found in his overcoat pocket? Couldn't the sender have dropped it in there while it was on the hook? It was cold Monday and Tuesday, both. What if someone put it there late Monday night or during rehearsal Tuesday morning?"

"Why, that seems pretty logical. But I can't see where it gets us. What if the killer did put it there? We know he got it to Schring some way."

"No, but I mean . . . it was seeing Bilbo that made me think of it. He dropped his mouthpiece into his pocket, to take home, you know. And it made Ralph— Mr. Payton—remember a time before, when he got home and found a mouthpiece in *his* pocket that wasn't his. Somebody had dropped it into the wrong pocket by mistake. You see?"

"I certainly do, but do you really think a murderer would be that careless?"

Nella said, "Probably not. Probably he was very careful to find the right hook. But, you see, Schring took a pride in just arriving in time for the downbeat. It was one of his little ways that drove the management so wild. Couldn't *he* have been careless about which hook he tossed his coat onto?"

Ross said, "This opens up a mighty interesting field of speculation, Miss Payne. I'm going to have to ask you to keep this conversation completely confidential. If it proves anything, if it leads anywhere, it could be dangerous for anybody to know you'd thought of it. You understand?"

Feeling as if an abyss had suddenly opened in front of her, Nella nodded. "I really do, Lieutenant. I won't say a word to anybody."

"Good girl." Ross watched her move off before he turned away himself. In turn, his departure was watched by a darker shadow pressed deep into the shadow cast by the looming harp case.

Nella found Angel, Lottie and Zaidee near the backstage exit. As she came near, Angel's whine rose shockingly on the ear.

"But it's twice as hard for me. Ronnie doesn't even get home until 5:30 or 6:00, and then I have to fix supper, and there's the kids! Why couldn't he just tell me, now?"

"A typical Manning stunt," snorted Lottie. "Keep 'em hanging till the last minute. He just enjoys having us come and beg."

Angel said, "Well, I simply can't go in there today. Funerals upset me so. I'm extra sensitive to emotional scenes. I've always been that way. Ronnie's always telling me to take it easy."

As Zaidee and Nella walked away from Angel's piercing complaints and Lottie's disgusted rumble, Zaidee explained, "It's Oscar being cute again. You've heard about that huge variety show Promate's sponsoring here in town to kick off their new sales campaign? Well, he's got the contract for the music, of course. They're calling it "A Thousand Strings"—so you know they'll begin by hiring all the Symphony violins and violas!

"But Oscar couldn't give anybody the satisfaction of saying, 'You're hired.' First, he waits till you come and ask about the show. Then he says, 'Well . . . I'll see if I can squeeze you in. Drop by my office in a day or two, in case I forget.' Smug little fink! Lottie's right—he dotes on being begged."

105

"Are you going by his office?"

"Not now. Later. Maybe tomorrow. Have to get my teeth set for it, you know, like biting into a lemon."

"Hi." Bill Buskirk, running a little late, hustled them and Ralph out to his car. "Sorry I'm late—had to see the lieutenant a minute."

Zaidee said, "Bill, we know you can't discuss the case with us, but for God's sake, tell us everything you can!"

He grinned, "Now that's about as tactful an inquiry as I've had in a long time. Thanks a lot, Zee. You were right the first time: I really can't talk about the case. Don't see how it can hurt, though, if I just mention that there isn't all that much not to talk about."

"You mean, you don't have any idea who did it?"

"You've got it," Ralph said. "Now look, Sis—all of you. It's only a couple of days since it happened. We're working on it. Eventually, in my opinion, we'll get the right answer. It's a hell of a lot better to go slowly than try to move too fast and wind up with a case of false arrest."

Nella said apologetically, "It seems as if it had happened a long time ago."

"That's because it was such a shock. Shock gets old in a hurry. Living with the idea that there's a murderer in the group wears on the nerves."

Ralph said, "Have you finished questioning everybody?"

"We've seen everybody once. We'll likely need to call some people back in. That's the way it's really done, you know, just keep hammering away. We sure didn't find any gold cigarette lighters or jade cuff links on the scene, so we'll just have to settle for good old police routine."

The little funeral home chapel was packed. Nearly all the Symphony musicians had come, partly out of respect for Milton and partly out of sympathy for Millie

Schring.

The minister seemed to be better acquainted with Millie than her husband, and he said as much during the brief sermon. He did manage, however, to usher Milton out of this world with a dignity that was both touching and consoling.

When her eye happened to fall on Buskirk, sitting beside her, Nella noticed that he was unobtrusively scanning the congregation, one row at a time. Following his glance, she noticed that at least two-thirds of the people at the funeral were women. Had he noticed that, too? That was in spite of the fact that the majority of Symphony personnel were men.

Millie Schring, the two daughters, an older woman, and some other relatives sat in an isolated clump in a partly concealed wing of the room. One of the girls was crying quietly, but Millie sat very still, her hands lying open on her lap.

At the graveside the ceremony also was brief. Masses of flowers remained to be placed around the new grave, and Nella had noticed a good many potted plants that very likely would be taken home for Millie. They stood back discreetly after the service, waiting their turns to shake hands with Millie. Zaidee exclaimed, "Good Lord! There's Mrs. Smallwood!"

Tottering determinedly across the uneven lawn, Verna Smallwood had taken off to reach Millie before either of the Lyles could help her. Spotting her takeoff after a momentary distraction, Helene Lyle said loudly, "Robert!" and snapped her fingers. Robert Lyle jumped to attendance on the little old figure as she reached her goal.

"Who is that?" murmured Nella, as much awed by the apparition itself as by Lyle's subservient attendance on it.

"That's our little annuity," said a voice behind them.

Oscar Manning had come up noiselessly. He nodded his head toward Millie and Mrs. Smallwood. "With any luck at all, when that old tabby has tottered into *her* grave, there'll be a sizeable endowment in her will for the orchestra."

Zaidee scolded, "That's no way to talk about her, Oscar. She's a real sweetheart. Gives a Christmas party for the kids under school age every year in her home—all the musicians' kids, I mean. They have a ball. We'll miss her horribly when she goes."

Manning rubbed his hands together, unimpressed by her disapproval. "Just the same, it's nice to know where the shekels are coming from. It's been announced publicly, or as good as. One of her lawyers 'leaked' the information after her will was made out, they say. Anyhow, she can hardly take it back now."

"Why would she want to? Her kids are grown and already provided for. Her husband's gone. And she lives for the Symphony. You don't know her," Zaidee added, turning to Nella and Ralph, "just because she's been ill this year. Heart trouble. This is the first season she's missed a concert since I don't know when."

"Do you suppose she ought to be here now?" Nella asked. "She looks so feeble. How old is she?"

"Over ninety. We gave her a big ninetieth birthday concert some years ago. Come on," Zaidee said suddenly, "let's move up while we can."

Manning already had circled around them and darted into the press of people. Now they saw him bowing low over Mrs. Smallwood's wrinkled paw. She stood for that, but when he ventured to take her by the elbow, she shook him off.

"Thank you, Mr. Manning, Robert will assist me," they heard her say grandly. "I want to go to the car now, Robert." Helene, trotting behind, slid into the back seat beside her. By insisting on using her own car,

108

Verna Smallwood kept them prisoners until she was disposed to return them to the hall.

"I'm glad there were lots of flowers," Nella said as they climbed back into the car. "When Millie thinks back about today, she'll be remembering all those beautiful arrangements, too."

"You're right, I think," Zaidee said. "They may not do any substantial good, but there's a comfort in them."

"Look, folks, I've got to eat," Bill said. "It may not be very appropriate, right on top of a funeral, but I'm starving, and God knows when I'll get off tonight."

"I'm hungry, too—I guess we all are," Nella said, gathering confirming nods, "but it does seem wrong to make an occasion of it. Could we just settle for hamburgers at a drive-in?"

They found a decent place on the way back and pulled in next to a familiar-looking blue sedan.

"Who's in that car?" Zaidee asked, craning to see. As the others turned to look, the driver of the blue car ground the starter into life and spurted away. The passenger in the seat beside him had a hand up shielding his face.

Ralph said, "Freed! Wasn't it? But why in the world would he race off like that? And who was that with him?"

Bill said drily, "Maybe he doesn't like eating next to the fuzz. Lots of people like that around. Seems to spoil their appetites."

"That's ridiculous," Zaidee snorted. "Could you see who the other guy was?"

"Couldn't see—but maybe I could guess."

"Who?"

"That's another thing I'm not talking about. If I'm right, it doesn't have anything to do with the murder, anyway."

"You're the most maddening brother! Maybe I don't like eating with the fuzz, either," sulked Zaidee.

While they waited for their orders, Ralph and Nella questioned Zaidee about some of the non-Symphony musicians who had attended the funeral. Both of them, being new, were largely unacquainted outside of the Symphony.

Milton had had his own little following among the League membership too, Zaidee explained. There had been a sprinkling of the very rich among the mourners. Most of them were people who had enjoyed Milton's artistry in small groups as well as in the orchestra. Like Nella, Zaidee had noticed the abundance of women in the crowd.

"You did recognize the gorgeous brunette in the navy-and-white suit and the huge navy hat, didn't you?"

"No, but she looked familiar. Who is she?"

"Just Nina Oldenberg."

"The oil heiress—really! An that was her husband with her. I remember now. They were at the concert Tuesday. In fact, they were there when the police came."

"Yes, that's her husband—her fourth. Not that Nina seems to make much distinction between the ones she's married to and the ones she isn't married to. She's got a real thing for a musical atmosphere, and doesn't seem to care who knows it. Didn't you see her glancing meaningfully at the great Robert Z, right in the middle of the eulogy?"

"Mr. Lyle! She wouldn't dare!"

"Better say, *he* wouldn't dare. Nina's a millionaire in her own right and can do what she damn well pleases. It's just the opposite with Lyle, so I hear. He doesn't dare put a foot wrong, because it's Mrs. who has the money."

Washing up in the women's room before time for the afternoon rehearsal, Zaidee and Nella met a beaming Evvie.

"I recognize the signs," Zaidee smiled, giving Evvie's delicately sloping shoulder a squeeze. "You've made up with the brute again."

"Oh, Zee, he's such a doll, really!" Evvie smiled delightedly as she corrected the arch of an eyebrow. "Would you believe he was worried that I might have come back to the Hall Tuesday night, and I was worried that he might have, and that's what the real trouble was?"

"All of which proves that neither of you did?"

"Well . . . not to say proves it to the police, exactly, but it does to our satisfaction."

Nella was baffled. "But what difference would it have made, if either one of you, or both of you, had come back? You certainly didn't suspect each other of the murder!"

"Oh, of course not. But don't you see, I didn't show up on stage with the people who were still in the Hall, and neither did he. So if either of us had gone back in and had not shown up, then everyone would think it looked like . . . like . . ."

"Hanky-panky," laughed Zaidee.

"Well, it sounds awfully silly when you just say it like that," admitted Evvie, laughing at herself, "but Toby is so . . . susceptible."

"Right on," Nella said approvingly. "Don't let Zaidee laugh you out of it. Don't let him get away with a thing."

Evvie said, "You'll be needing to take some of your own advice soon, Nella. That horn player is getting pretty interested, isn't he? How about you—is the attraction mutual?"

Caught off base, Nella felt her neck and face go red.

"Oh, it's too early to think about. Ralph is an interesting person, though. I think we have a lot in common."

"Famous last words," groaned Zaidee and Evvie, almost together.

Swinging the door wide as they left the room, they almost collided with Lottie Williams. Startled, the three of them stepped out of the way and were more startled by the way Lottie brushed past without a word. Lottie was not a woman to lose an opportunity for words with almost any listener.

"Now, what's she up to?" Nella wondered aloud as the door swung closed.

"Combing her hair, I hope," Evvie muttered. "I swear it was sticking straight out."

Zaidee said charitably, "Maybe the funeral upset her."

"Something has," Nella said. "Well, see you after a while. I need to warm up before the downbeat."

CHAPTER XI

When they were settled in Lyle's office again after a visit to headquarters, Ross questioned Buskirk about the funeral. Had anyone said or done anything unusual? Was anyone there, or not there, so as to be surprising?

Buskirk spread a large, well-shaped hand, palm up. "Looked above-board as far as I could tell, Lieutenant. I know most of the older Symphony hands; Zee drags me out to their social occasions once or twice a year, anyway. All the ones I'd most expect to be there showed up. Some people might think it was unusual for Verna Smallwood to be there, but I think it's just the kind of thing she would do. To me it was more surprising that the Lyles condescended to come. Somehow, I don't think they would've been there if she hadn't put the pressure on."

Ross dismissed the topic. He tapped a paper in front of him that contained several columns of hand-written names and times. "Somehow I think this is going to be a water haul, too, but let's see if we can't eliminate *somebody* on the grounds of physical impossibility."

Able made a discouraging noise in his throat, but he pulled up a chair on the other side of Buskirk and fixed his baby blue eyes on the paper.

Ross pointed his pencil at the first column. "There's Lyle. Waiting in the wings for the conductor in sight of twenty or so people. Grabbed him and walked off with him. We've finally found out when exactly Trevelyn's driver came for him. It had to be between 11:30 and 11:35. No sooner, no later."

Able said, "Then doesn't that eliminate Lyle, after all? We agree, don't we, that the murder has to have been done at least by 11:30?"

"Let's call it a seventy-five percent possibility, anyway. McCord and that other hand both say the wrist and hand had begun to cool by 11:45. Of course, that part of the backstage hall is pretty cool at this time of year. They'd turned off the central heat, too, by eleven, don't forget."

"Then can we scratch off Lyle?" Buskirk asked.

"Not quite," Ross said. "He mentioned to me that the conductor stepped into the private bathroom connected to the Mauve Room sometime during their visit. I know, I know, it doesn't seem likely he'd take the risk, but it's *possible*."

"Who's next?" Able asked.

"Oscar Manning." The pencil jumped down a line.

"My pick for the job," Buskirk growled. "Don't tell me he's alibied for the whole half-hour."

"No way," Ross said sadly. "I wish somebody was! He says he was in the crowd Trevelyn walked into after the concert. Probably he was, but people we've asked are so used to seeing him here, there, and everywhere, they don't really notice when he's there and when he's not. Anyway, he says that he waited for Nella to come off. Wanted to give the little girl a treat, is the way he put it. Took her to meet the big man.

"After she took off as soon as she was introduced, he left the Mauve Room. From that point on, he gets completely vague. Incredibly so, in fact. Talked to so many people, he couldn't possibly remember who they were or in what sequence he saw them. I don't buy it, but I can't shake him. He was up to something. Trouble with Manning seems to be, he's always up to something. What was it this time?"

"Pushing that weight off the ladder," Buskirk said.

Ross said, "Now we come to Millie Schring. She was in Ohio, that's been checked. Our first complete alibi—maybe our only one. Even the ones who left immediately after the concert can't be crossed off. With that damned door unlocked, there was nothing to prevent anyone from slipping back in and pushing off the weight. I guess we're spinning our wheels."

"Have you got that Williams dame down there?" Able asked. "She acts so damn fishy, she's gotta be hiding something."

Ross waved away the thought. "She's a type; the conspiratorial female. Everything's got to be a secret. She always latches onto one or two bosom friends and confides in them. Can't walk into a room without bustling up to somebody and telling a deep, dark secret."

Buskirk nodded. "Whether she has a secret to tell at that moment, or not. I know what you mean. Zee tolerates her better than most people do. She's often the one Lottie confides in. Never amounts to a hill of beans."

"Nevertheless," Ross said, "let's see what we can prove as to her whereabouts . . . not much. She's wide open until 11:25, or it may be 11:30. Says she never glanced at her watch, of course. Somewhere about then she grabbed Angel Angelo—Able, make sure I get that woman's first name from somewhere! They wound up having coffee with Julius Oldenberg. She was still with him at 11:45 when they rounded up everybody after the body was found."

Able said incredulously, "*Alone* with him?"

Ross chuckled. "Didn't start out that way. Lottie and this Angel were sitting there, so it seems, and he came up and sat with them. Why not? The Angelo dame's gorgeous until she opens her mouth. Very likely he'd never happened to meet her before. Must have been quite a shock when she said hello."

Able grinned, "When she said anything. I keep thinking she's putting me on."

"We can suppose he thought so. Anyway, she'd about finished, and left for home just a few minutes before the hand came in to get everybody."

"What about Freed?" asked Buskirk.

"Seen in the bar across the street almost immediately after the concert. Apparently several of the musicians made a beeline for it—one or two notable soaks, the honeymoon couple—"

"What honeymoon couple?"

"Oh, they aren't married, really. I've been thinking of them that way because of the way they act," Ross said easily. "The big fellow, Toby somebody, and that old-fashioned looking girl. Plays first viola. What's her name? Evvie."

"They saw Freed?" Able put in.

"Yes, but not long enough to eliminate him. He was still there when they had their spat and both took off in separate directions. By the way, Bilbo Jones mentioned that to me. He said each of them, the couple, I mean, was worried that the other one could have gone back into the Hall. Jones took that to mean that neither one of them had."

"Not necessarily," Buskirk said.

"I know," Ross said. "But frankly, I don't have the ghost of a reason to think either of them attacked Schring. For what reason? There's just no provable connection."

"Wait a minute," Able said. "Freed said that Schring made a pass at this Evvie in the bar."

"Standard operating procedure," Ross said, "or so I have been told. But we can't even eliminate them. I've got a good mind to dump this whole sheet into the wastebasket." He waved it in disgust.

"Please don't do that, Lieutenant," Able said, alarmed. "I'd just have to make another one for the record."

Buskirk said, "You were going to explain what this Payne girl was telling you before? About the coat hooks?"

"Oh, yes," growled Ross. "Another complication. Seems that Schring might not have been the intended victim at all." He explained how the note might have gotten into Schring's pocket by mistake.

"Then, my God, can't we find out who had the hooks close to him?" Able exclaimed.

"We'll find out," Ross told him. "I've already asked Manning, the great executive, who has the list. Of course he had to make the point that he can't be bothered by petty details like that. Suggested we try McCord. He knows as much as anybody about physical arrangements backstage."

"Shall I get McCord for you?" Buskirk asked.

"I've already spoken to him once. He was going to get me this list right away. That was before the funeral, and it's still not here. We may have to jump him again."

"Don't suppose there's any checking up on McCord's own movements during that time, is there?" Buskirk asked.

"Don't ask," Ross said gloomily. "Let's get on with the interviews. I'd like to finish up here and get back downtown in the next hour or so, if we can. Able, who do I have to see next?"

"Mrs. Angelo," Able said, consulting his notebook.

"Oh, God," Ross groaned, "how much of that whine can I take?"

"Look on the bright side," Buskirk suggested. "Now you can find out what her first name is."

"Well, get her," Ross said to Able. "I hear them tuning up now. Better pull her out before rehearsal begins."

The afternoon rehearsal took up most of the short winter daylight hours. Nella, who had promised to wait through the section rehearsal for second fiddles and to take Zaidee home with her for supper, had brought a book.

Ralph followed her offstage, wanting to know if she needed a ride home.

"No, thanks. I've got my car. It's Zaidee who needs transportation, but I'm waiting for her to get through the section rehearsal. I'm taking her home for dinner."

"Are you?" He made such an obvious effort to look wistful and famished at the same time that Nella had to laugh.

"Sure you don't need any masculine company this evening? Neither of you girls nervous? I'm not so great as a fighter, but my size'd scare off fifty percent of your ordinary hoods."

A momentary remembrance of that peculiar phone call the night before flashed through her mind, but Nella shook it away. Just a silly person who'd tried to play a practical joke. What else could it have been?

"Another time, we'll try your services," Nella promised. "This is strictly a hen party."

"What are you going to do right now—just wander around the backstage till she's finished?"

"I meant to find a cozy spot and read, but somehow I can't seem to settle down. Sample said he's going to be back here, somewhere, changing heads on his timpani. I thought I might try to talk to him."

"Don't try it—you might find a fate worse than death!"

"Good Lord, you don't mean he's another Casanova!"

"Just the opposite. When he gets strung out messing with those kettles, he changes into a werewolf at the merest sign of an interruption."

"What! Nice old mild-mannered Sample? You're joking! Why, I've never heard him utter a cross word to anybody."

"You've never seen him changing heads, either. Once was enough for me. Well, if you won't be warned, I'm off. You'll be sorry you didn't invite me to supper if I starve to death. See you in the morning."

Nella, smiling him away, decided he must have been exaggerating about Sample. Instead of resembling Thor, the Thunderer, Sample was one timpanist who seemed more like a genial sun-god, beaming friendly acceptance on all within his radius. She'd go have a pleasant visit with him while he worked.

She heard him before she saw him, crouched like a spider in the center of newspapers spread out in a wide area backstage. He was rumbling steadily like distant thunder, reciting a monotonous string of curses. The great copper kettledrum in front of him was stripped naked, an open cauldron with only a "spider"—the pedal tuning device—in the center at the bottom of the kettle.

On the newspaper were the gleaming rim that held in place the enormous drum head, the discarded head itself, six steel rods that fitted into the rim at even intervals, an open can of lighter fluid, an open jar of Vaseline, some rags, and a large thin square box which she supposed held the new drum head. Garnet paper in one hand and rag in the other, Sample was burnishing the edge of the kettle.

Finding that saying "hello" two or three times brought no response, Nella watched silently for a moment. Just as Sample picked up the lighter fluid to douse his rag again, she said, "Want some help? I'm a pretty good scrubber."

It must have been the first time Sample had been

aware of anyone. He jumped violently, jerking the fluid can so that a large splash jumped out of the can and fell onto his suede shoe. "Oh, *hell*," he roared, dabbing violently at the spill.

"Oh, I'm sorry! Here, let me . . ." Nella stepped forward, reaching for a rag.

Sample writhed away in an agony of apprehension. "*Don't step on my head*," he moaned.

Offended, Nella stopped dead still. "I am not stepping on anything but the floor," she said loudly and clearly.

Sample pulled the timpanum toward him in a convulsive, protective gesture. An explosive silence fell.

Nella had "her ears back" now, as her mother used to say. She was determined to make him say a civil word. "What do you call that one?" she asked sweetly.

"Arrr—whaddya mean, call it?"

"Well, you have four timpani. You must call each one of them something, don't you, to know which one you're talking about?"

Sample gave her a red-eyed glare, as if the rocks in her head must be visible. "This is the twenty-six-inch one," he said, enunciating very carefully, as one would for a feeble-minded person, "and I don't usually have to talk about them."

"Oh." Defeated, she made a hasty retreat into the Mauve Room. There she curled up on the sofa. The door was slightly ajar so she could tell by the distant music when the section rehearsal was over.

When a thudding silence fell, Nella told herself that the conductor was talking something over with the fiddle players, but she couldn't subdue a creeping feeling of isolation. I should go sit at a stage entrance to wait, she told herself. A kind of stubborn pride kept her where she was. This hall was her home away from home; she refused to be afraid in it.

She had just settled into the book when Freed glided into the room. He looked so startled at the sight of Nella that she wanted to laugh. Trying, and failing, to think what his first name was, she said, "Hi, there. Are you waiting for somebody, too? Plenty of chairs here. Come in and be comfortable."

"No—no, of course not! You haven't seen anyone, I mean, has anyone come in?"

"I've only been here a few minutes. Waiting for Zaidee Buskirk. Whom did you want to see?"

"Nothing—nobody. Of course not!" Freed departed as suddenly as he had come.

Her novel was a well-researched historical one, set in the medieval period she loved, but it didn't hold her attention this afternoon. She found herself re-reading pages she had gone over without paying attention. It was more interesting to speculate about the murder.

What in the world was scaring Freed so badly? He'd been nervous as a cat ever since Ross had first questioned him. Surely he couldn't have brought himself to an act of violence just to get the principal chair. Besides, maybe Schring wasn't even meant to be the victim. If the note had been dropped into the wrong coat pocket, then Schring might have been murdered by mistake.

Was it possible? Yes, the spot where it had happened was dark. He had been, she understood, standing still with his back to the killer. The intended victim only needed to be a man of about the same height. And, of course, wearing tails. Any difference might not have been noticed as the deadly weight had been nudged loose. Especially as the murderer may have been in a hurry . . .

When the violins stopped momentarily for the leader to make a point, silence wrapped the room. How still it was with all the other players gone!

A creak. Was it? A mouse. No, another creak. The

old hall was settling down for the evening, surely . . no. A footstep. The door swung a few inches, then fully open. Oscar stood there frowning.

She watched his expression move from simple surprise to annoyance in remembrance of his rebuff last Tuesday night. She had had to reject him pretty rudely to make him see her point.

"Well, so it's little Nell! I wondered who'd left the light on in here. Waiting for someone?" He was going to be nasty-nice, which suited Nella much better than his amorous routine.

"For Zaidee."

"How cozy. I thought maybe that policeman was still around. He's been cluttering up Lyle's office all day. Noticed you buttering him up at the coffee break this morning. How do you know he's not married and the papa of twins?"

She reflected how easy it was to tell by Manning's attitude exactly where one stood on his ladder of importance. For enemies who mattered, he had a rapier; for unimportant persons like her, a bludgeon would do. She hadn't been going to answer, but then a thought struck her.

"Oscar, where do you hang your coat? I mean, what number did you draw?"

"I don't draw numbers," he said loftily. "I simply reserve the first five blue ones for times when it's not convenient to get to my office. Why? Has some fool gotten my place again?"

"I don't know . . . do you mean someone used your hook before?"

"Some jerk is always doing it. Nearly got off with his coat the other morning. Looked just like mine, except for the lining, and my name's sewn in. Lucky I noticed. Seen Regal around? He's got the list. Might as well find out now who's been doing it."

She hadn't seen Regal, and said no, and Manning left. Luckily, he seemed to have forgotten that Nella had brought up the subject and she had never explained why. She'd remembered in time that Ross had said not to mention it to anyone. Nella thought of phoning Ross with this tidbit, and decided it would seem like minding his business for him. After all, his investigators would ferret out all these details. And if Manning couldn't remember which day the mixup had happened, it might prove nothing at all.

But she thought, all at once, how easy it would be to find suspects if Manning had been supposed to be the victim! On second thought, it was a horrible idea. There was no one—literally no one—in the orchestra as Nella knew it who might *not* be suspected of killing Manning. Well, of course, except Ralph. And, say, the three or four others who were new within the past six months.

All the others had cause to dislike, hate, and resent the executive secretary. In some cases, he interfered with people's lives by controlling their extra work. In others, he exercised a talent for petty tyranny that kept the more vulnerable ones feeling diminished and infuriatingly put down.

There was another visitor, just as Nella was settling down again. It was Pete Rollinson. Nella had become friends with Pete, limp wrist and all, because Ralph liked him. She had asked Zaidee not long ago if perhaps Pete's effeminate physical mannerisms hadn't made people misjudge him.

"Poor old Pete? Oh, I'm pretty sure he's queer as a three-dollar bill. What I admire about him is the way he keeps his private life really private. You never see him trying to convert anybody else to his tastes. He just lives in peace and harmony with his roommate. You can invite him to your parties or not, and he'll still be your friend. And he really has an interesting mind."

Smiling now at the willowy form in the doorway, Nella asked, "Looking for someone, Pete?"

"Why, not really," Pete murmured. "Just seeing who was here. Look out for Sample when you leave. He's on the warpath."

"I know, I know . . . changing heads. I made the mistake of speaking to him," she laughed.

"Oh, well, at least he's Dr. Jekyll ninety-nine percent of the time, and Mr. Hyde only one percent," Pete said. "Is that a good book, Nella?"

They talked authors for a while. Pete gave her a graceful wave and left. She read a little longer and then decided the section rehearsal must be about over. She stepped into the backstage gloom, turning off the light at the door as she came out.

Reflected light from the stage shone dimly down the passage to her right. Out of the darkness on her left, something suddenly loomed up at her side. She heard a maniacal laugh.

Rooted to the floor, a prisoner of her own terror, Nella screamed. A gloved hand reached out toward her as she blacked out.

CHAPTER XII

"Nella! Nella! Where is she?" Zaidee ran along the backstage ahead of a startled group of violinists. Lights jumped on to reveal Nella, supported by an embarrassed Regal, struggling to gather her wits again.

"My God, how you scared us! Are you all right? What happened?"

Regal thankfully turned her over to her friends. "My fault, I guess," he admitted sullenly. "Thought I'd just surprise her, you know, just a friendly little joke," he went on.

"He jumped at me," Nella said, "and laughed . . . did I scream? I thought I couldn't scream or move, or anything. I'm sorry . . . so silly of me."

"Did you scream! It was high E, at least. Damn it, Regal, you ought to have had better sense!" But he was already disappearing down the exit stairs. Zaidee was still sputtering indignation as they returned for her instrument and left the hall.

"Remember, I'm sitting right beside you all the way home," she told Nella in the parking lot. "Thank God we planned to get together this evening anyway." Bill would come to pick up his sister around ten o'clock or when he got off duty, if it was later.

Nella echoed that thought in her mind as she drove home extra carefully. It was a fact that her coordination was off; her hand still shook. Never mind. A cheerful evening with Zaidee would take care of that.

They took their time getting the meal together, sipping Scotch and water and generally unwinding. They had just sat down to bacon quiche and salad and iced tea when someone pounded vigorously on the kitchen door. "Someone who knows you," Zaidee observed quickly. "They've used your stairs."

Through the yellow nylon curtain that draped the window in the upper door, Nella spotted an unmistakeable profile. "It's Lottie," she moaned over her shoulder.

Lottie was talking before she crossed the threshold. ". . . and I'm sorry to barge in like this, Nella, but when you screamed like that and fainted at the section rehearsal . . . well, not at it, you know, but backstage like that, I just knew you'd guessed the same thing I have . . . well, not guessed, you know, but practically iron clad evidence, if you know the characters involved as well as we do, and besides, didn't I hear them myself, going at it hammer and tongs, right after the concert, which is to say, right before the murder, and if that doesn't prove it, well, what more could anyone want?"

She nodded around significantly from Zaidee to Nella and back. Nella found herself nodding in reply, not having the foggiest notion what she was replying to.

Zaidee was more accustomed to the Williams style of address. She said crisply, "What the hell are you talking about, Lottie?"

"*You* know." Lottie shot a conspiratorial glance toward Zaidee, but then thought better of it and shifted her focus to Nella. "Nella knows. Or why did she really scream like that? Nella knows."

Her voice had sunk to a semi-whisper. When both her listeners still looked mystified, she added, "It was *Regal*!"

"I know," Nella said. "Didn't you hear him admit it? He just hid behind the harp case and jumped out to scare me. It was just a stupid joke. I really think he was sorry about it."

Lottie had sat down at the dining table where the quiche was slowly cooling. She slammed her hand down on the cloth with a bang that made the silverware jump. "No, no, no! I don't mean *that* was Regal, well, of course it was, but I don't mean *that*! I mean . . . don't you really know?"

"Know what, for Pete's sake, Lottie? If you've really got something to tell, tell it!" snapped Zaidee.

Lottie's button-black eyes sparkled with satisfaction. She had hoped, but not really expected, that her story would be news to both of them. She let her face assume a tragic look. "It was Regal who dropped that weight on Schring."

Nella said, "How do you know that?"

Zaidee said, "Did you see him? Because if you didn't, you're making a very serious accusation, Lottie. I really think . . ."

"I heard them! Not then, of course—there wasn't any talking to it when he dropped that weight. But before—earlier, right after the concert, they were quarreling at the tops of their lungs."

"Shouting? Really? Why in the world didn't anyone else hear them?" Zaidee asked.

"No, not shouting—except in whispers, because they didn't want anyone to hear them—but they were both whispering louder and louder because they were so mad. They were *whispering* at the tops of their lungs," Lottie said with wounded dignity.

"Sounds pretty crazy to me," Nella said. "Why would they want to quarrel in whispers?"

"Because the maestro and Lyle were moseying around backstage, and you know how mad the management gets if we ever let a visiting conductor see any friction going on," Lottie said.

There was truth in that, to be sure. Lyle and Manning insisted on a smooth, unruffled surface to be presented to the outside world at all times. The orchestra might be, and occasionally was, a hotbed of dissension. Mix ninety-odd artists of any type together, and sparks will tend to fly. Nothing but sweet harmony must be heard outside the orchestra itself. Regal and Schring would have had to answer for quarreling in the presence of a guest conductor.

"And then what?" Zaidee wanted to know.

Lottie looked at her blankly. "That's all."

"But what happened after you heard them quarreling? Did you go off and leave them at it? Did they leave together, or what?"

"Oh, Regal stormed off. He was still muttering to himself. And Schring just stood there for a minute. He looked at his watch."

Nella was getting the picture. "And then you left?"

Lottie said, "Yes. But Regal must have come back sometime in the next half hour, still mad, and knocked that weight down. What else makes sense?"

"Did you hear what they were saying to each other at all?" Zaidee asked.

Reluctantly, Lottie said, "Well, not a lot. But I think Regal was mad because of the night before. Remember, Milton was just at downbeat getting into his chair? And he'd parked right where Regal puts his truck, out by the stage door. He knew better than to do that. When he was late, he'd have to sometimes, to make one of those last-minute entrances of his. Probably, Regal couldn't catch him to fuss at the night before, so last night he let him have it."

Lottie, unconscious of the dreadful double meaning of her last words, paused to enjoy the satisfaction of being taken quite seriously by her audience.

Zaidee was weighing the possibilities. "But that's so

trivial. Nobody kills a man just because of a little thing like his car being in the way!"

"*You* wouldn't. *I* wouldn't. But how do you know what a moron like Regal might do? It wasn't just once that we're talking about. It was time and time again, one little irritation after another, and Milton always acting too good to see Regal when he'd come to complain, you know how he did, and Regal may be dumb, but he's got his pride, in fact, which is to say, his conceit, and how do you know how all that would've built up over the years? And besides, he's just dumb enough to have thought it wouldn't kill him, just give him a good knock, like teach him a lesson, you know?"

It seemed faintly possible to Nella, especially after Regal's bad joke of that afternoon. Moronic he certainly was. Couldn't he have been too stupid to guess a crack on the head like that would kill Schring? But still . . . "No, Lottie, it's just too much. How can you believe that anybody—even Regal, would murder for reasons like that?"

Lottie quivered with the pleasure of delivering her final bombshell. "Well, if he didn't do it, *why is he being blackmailed*?"

At the end of her tolerance, Zaidee bristled. "Now, Lottie!"

"No, I mean it!" Listen, you know those two pay phone booths that are close to the backstage door? They're built together in one unit. Remember how that tenor got upset over something last year and put his fist right through the dividing partition between them? Well, there's just a little sheet of black plastic covering that hole, and you can't help but hear what a person in the other booth is saying."

"You mean, you got into the other booth and listened to Regal talking to somebody?"

It was too obvious for denials; if Regal had seen that

someone was in the other booth before he had phoned, he would have waited for privacy. Lottie must have slipped into the adjoining booth to listen.

"I had to telephone my aunt," she said with dignity. "I heard him! I distinctly heard him say, 'The truth about Schring,' and 'All right, then, I'll meet you down there at six-forty-five. Don't be late.' He sounded mad, all right."

"It's past that now," Zaidee observed sarcastically. "Guess we've missed a golden opportunity of catching a murderer and blackmailer red-handed. Seriously, Lottie, the whole thing is just too thick to believe. Probably those words you overheard, if they were put back into context, would mean something else entirely. Anyway, I certainly wouldn't repeat them to anybody else if I were you."

Her bombshell exploded, Lottie soon bustled off into the chilly evening. Nella and Zaidee divided their attention between the meal and circuitous speculations.

"This is the great comfort of having Bill for a brother," Zaidee said. "I'll just dump all this talk into his lap, and he'll know how to sort it out. Then I can forget about it."

Nella asked, "Are you going to tell him everything Lottie said?"

"Oh, yes. He knows, by now, whether she ought to be taken seriously or not. And I'll tell him, too, about that silly joke Regal played on you. He can decide whether to tell the lieutenant."

After dinner, they declared a truce to conversation about the murder and managed to enjoy the rest of the evening listening to the stereo and chatting over their personal concerns.

Facing Lieutenant Ross in Lyle's office next morning, Regal McCord had to explain his joke on Nella once more. "Didn't expect the silly dame to come unglued," he muttered. "Hell, those musicians are always playing jokes on each other."

"That may be so," Ross said mildly, "but I doubt if many of them would have considered making that kind of joke right after a murder had been committed."

Regal grew more defensive. "Well, what difference does that make to her? She have something to do with it? You don't know these secton players like I do, Lieutenant. Get sort of nutty, after a while.

"They work too close to each other, see? Like, they've got stand partners, see; it's one guy's turn to turn the page while the other guy plays a solo. So he wants to make the soloist look bad. He's just a little slow getting the page turned, or he picks up two pages at once—you'd be surprised the tricks they do."

"Schring and Miss Payne weren't stand partners."

"Oh, hell no! She's brand new—just got out of the conservatory year before last. But she's in the same *section*, see? And they get all kinds of jealousies and competitions going. I'm just tellin' you, they're all too close to each other. Get to know each other too well. So why's Miss Nice Nellie so nervous? Maybe she knows too much."

Ross's green eyes glittered. "McCord, what do you mean, exactly: Knows too much about what?"

McCord said, "Well, why'd she jump and scream just because someone come up unexpected? Maybe she knows who done the murder."

Ross said, "What evidence do you have that Miss Payne knows anything in paticular?"

McCord said desperately, "Well, I heard *him* with my own ears, and that's a fact. Heard him tell her 'see you later.' "

"Who is 'him?' "

"Schring, of course!"

"When was this? Be careful, now, I want the exact

time, near as you can come."

"Hell, that's easy. It was right before the concert, Tuesday night."

"What did she say to him?"

"Well, nothing, I guess. Anyway, I didn't hear her say nothing. She had her back to me, but if she'd said anything. I'd probably have heard it. She might of just winked or nodded."

"I don't get the picture. Weren't they having a regular conversation?"

"Naw. She and Zaidee'd been talking. That's when Schring walks by, and he says to her, 'see you later.' I heard him, plain as I hear you now. His exact words: 'see you later.'"

Ross said, "All right. Now are you claiming this is evidence in the murder, because you could tell, somehow, from those three words, that he was making a date with Miss Payne for after the concert?"

That was farther than McCord intended to go. "Didn't say I had no evidence," he said. "Just seemed peculiar, her getting so nervous and all."

Ross kept his temper. "I hope you don't intend to repeat any suspicious remarks like that, McCord, unless you're prepared to back up what you say with solid facts," he said. "By the way, did you bring me that list I asked you for yesterday?"

"What list?"

"Of the coat hook assignments—who drew what hook in what color section this year. You said there was just the one list, and you'd bring it to me. Where is it?"

"Oh, that. Tell you want—I haven't come across it yet. Keep it in a desk in the property room generally, but it don't seem to be there. I'll get it for you today, first chance I get." He clomped out, cowboy boots tapping along to a fast fadeout toward the rehearsing orchestra.

Ross caught Nella on her way out after the rehearsal.

"Are you going home now, Miss Payne?"

"Yes, we don't rehearse this afternoon."

"I've taken the liberty of sending for a couple of corned beef on ryes from the delicatessen," he told her. "Don't have time to go out for lunch. I was hoping you'd join me so we could cover a few points that have come up."

"Well, thanks. Of course." She followed him into the office without enthusiasm.

While they ate, Ross led her to talk about her impressons as a new member of the orchestra. Just as they finished, he asked, "Who's the biggest gossip in the orchestra, Miss Payne?"

"It'd be a toss-up between Lottie Williams and Regal McCord."

"But McCord's just a stagehand, isn't he?"

"Oh, yes, but there aren't those kinds of social distinctions. I mean, there are—we tend to run in cliques, I'm afraid—but one person's gossip is as good as another's. Or," she laughed, "as bad—well, you see what I mean."

Ross fixed his green gaze steadily on her. "Does this phrase mean anything special to you: 'see you later'?"

"Oh! Who told you that?" She knew by the feel of her skin that her face had gone pale.

"Why? What does it mean to you, Miss Payne?"

"Nothing! Except that somebody, I thought a joker or a wrong number, called me a couple of nights ago and said that, and hung up."

"Couldn't you recognize the voice?"

"It was disguised. I know because at first I didn't understand a single word, so I said I didn't understand, and then the voice changed from muffled to high-pitched, but it was still disguised, and it said the same words."

"And the words didn't mean anything special to

133

you?"

"Not at the time. Since then, Ralph—Ralph Payton —has reminded me who said them to me Tuesday night."

"Regal McCord says that's what Milton Schring said to you just before the concert Tuesday. Probably the last words he ever said to you, wouldn't they be?"

"Yes. So that's why . . . it must have been Regal on the phone! But he didn't mean anything—Milton, I mean."

Ross said gently, "He must have meant something, don't you think?"

"Well, I remember, Zaidee asked me what he meant at the time. I really didn't know, so I said he must have meant the overture that we were playing."

Ross said, "Could he have been reminding you to meet him after the concert, Miss Payne?"

Nella gave him a long, straight stare. "Lieutenant Ross. I don't have any idea how to make you believe me. I don't know why Milton Schring said that. I didn't make a date with him; I didn't meet him; I didn't kill him. Why in the world would I?"

Ross told her frankly that McCord had hinted Nella might know more than she should about last Tuesday night. Nella told him again that she hadn't even remembered Schring's speaking to her before the concert until Ralph had reminded her. Ross asked, "Do you think McCord has some grudge against you, Miss Payne?"

Earlier, she had been on the point of breaking the awkward formality by saying that Ross should call her Nella, but somehow the turn his questions had taken made such freedom impossible.

"Regal? Oh, no. They told me about him when I first came here. He just can't keep himself from making innuendoes. He's a natural conspirator. Today I'm the victim; probably he's a little miffed because his silly joke backfired yesterday. Tomorrow, he'll be making sly suggestions against somebody else."

"But his calling you at home, at night, and saying those words? What do you make of that?"

"Not too much. Regal is pretty dim mentally, you know. I can imagine him having a few beers and deciding to play detective. Maybe he thought I'd say something incriminating on the phone."

"You don't take him seriously at all?"

"Why, no. Basically, I think he's harmless. He'll be picking on someone else tomorrow or the next day."

"But for now, he's likely to spread the word that you know something about the murder. Don't you think, Miss Payne, that that might be dangerous for you—the wrong person hears him, and takes him more seriously than you do?"

"Why, I don't know. All right, I don't like it, but how can I stop him?"

Ross was grim. "I don't think you can. That's why, although God knows it's hard to spare the extra man, I mean to assign someone to keep an eye on you. For the present, anyway. Starting tomorrow."

CHAPTER XIII

Zaidee had "psyched" herself into going alone to Manning's office after rehearsal that morning. She needed to ask about the "Thousand Strings" job. It would mean at least three nights' work, with possibly two two-hour daytime rehearsals. There was one good thing about having Oscar do the booking: work schedules on these extra jobs never conflicted with Symphony hours. He saw to that.

Manning's office was a small, neat room on the floor just below the ground floor. The second basement was occupied by storerooms, maintenance areas, and the music library.

Also on the floor with Manning's office was the big rehearsal room the orchestra had used two days this week, so that the stage could be occupied by a traveling show. Zaidee could see the rehearsal room door just beyond Manning's office as she approached, tapping along in the high heels she loved to wear. It crossed her mind vaguely that the rehearsal room door seemed just to have shut. She wondered, idly, who had left some belonging there and returned for it. She stopped at Manning's door and knocked. No answer. Turning the knob, she found the door unlocked. She pushed it open and felt for the light switch on the wall.

The room was in shambles. It seemed almost as if someone had planned, insanely, to make a bonfire in the middle of the carpeted floor. Every paper that had been in or on the desk was dumped in a heap on the floor. Desk drawers hung open, except for the left-hand bottom one, which remained undisturbed. Two drawers had been pulled out and thrown down on the heap of papers.

A smaller litter of envelopes, letters, and bills trailed toward the deep storage closet on one side of the back wall. The other side held a closed door that led to a tiny private bathroom.

· Zaidee looked about for Manning. When had she seen him last? Had he—how could he—have done this? Surely not! It was sheer vandalism or something. Without consciously thinking about it, she stooped and began to straighten the smaller heap of papers.

Without noise, the rehearsal room door opened and shut again. A figure glided into Manning's office doorway, took in the stooping shape of Zaidee reaching for papers. Taking its time, the shadow lifted a stiff hand and brought it down edgewise on Zaidee's neck. She fell soundlessly. The shadow reached for the bottom desk drawer, began to go quickly but carefully through its contents.

Having fortified herself after rehearsal with a cup of coffee and a gossip with Angel, Lottie Williams braced herself to beard Manning in his den.

"Sure you don't want to go with me?" she asked Angel.

"No, thanks! Once is enough. The little jerk acted as if he were throwing me a crust of bread when I asked him for myself. I can't stand that little creep. Why don't you see if Zaidee wants to go with you?"

"You and me both," groaned Lottie. "Zaidee's disappeared somewhere. Maybe she's already asking. I hate to be last."

She took the nearer stairs down to the first basement.

From a distance she saw Manning's door open and the light was on. At least she wouldn't have to wait for him to show up.

Lottie's crepe soles made no noise on the floor. The dark figure she saw bending over Zaidee had no warning of her approach. Everything flashed on her eyes at once: Zaidee unconscious, the menacing shape above her, the open closet door, a plain old-fashioned key on its outside. Lottie took instinctive, heroic action.

She half jumped, half fell against the dark figure, shoved it into the closet, and the closet door shut at the same time. She turned the key in the lock. When the key was safely in her hand, she started screaming and ran down the hall.

Ross and Nella heard the commotion from Lyle's office on the ground floor as Lottie came wailing out of the stairwell.

"He's killed Zaidee! She's lying there. I saw her! Oh, my God, he's killed her!" In the grip of hysteria, Lottie shook her head from side to side, avoiding Ross's restraining hands.

Bill Buskirk materialized beside the screaming woman. He slapped her hard, twice. She gasped and quieted down.

"Where is she?" he demanded.

Lottie held up the closet key. "Down there . . . in Manning's office . . . I locked him in the closet."

Trembling, Nella put an arm around her. "First you said it was Zaidee, now you say it's him. Who's down there, Lottie? Who's in Manning's office?"

"No, no! Zaidee's on the floor . . . there in the office . . . but *he* was stooping over her. I pushed him into the closet. I locked him in." The beginning of pride crept into Lottie's voice as she started to regain her composure and realize what she had done.

"Hadn't we better . . ." Nella turned to say to Ross

and Buskirk, but they were long gone. She turned back to Lottie, who was clinging to her. "I've got to go to see about her, Lottie," she said.

"Don't leave me! Oh, don't go down there! They'll go—they have to—it's their job. Let them go! It's horrible. Oh, don't go!"

Nella was shaking all over; she didn't know if it was from inside herself, or because Lottie was trembling. "I have to, Lottie. And you shouldn't be here by yourself. Come with me. We'll be all right together; come on. You don't have to come all the way; just come down into the hall nearby. You won't have to go in there again."

Finally, Lottie went with Nella, slowly, protesting all the way, dragging her feet. They were still yards from the open office door when Ross looked out and saw them coming.

"She's all right," he called.

Warm relief swept over Nella so that she clung to Lottie a minute before her knees remembered to function. She dragged Lottie on. They couldn't have entered the tiny office if they had wanted to. Zaidee, sitting in Manning's posture chair, glanced toward them groggily. Bill crouched beside his sister, murmuring to her urgently. The pile of litter took up all the floor space in front of the desk.

Ross, a gun in his right hand, approached the closet door with the key extended in his left. Suddenly, a new noise halted them all in their tracks.

It was a furious pounding from inside the closet. A voice, strident but recognizable, accompanied the banging. "Let me out! Who's out there? Open this door! Get the police! Let me out! Who's . . ."

Ross opened the door.

Oscar Manning, long strands of hair dangling in his eyes, blood running freely from a cut on the right temple, bounded out furiously. He stopped dead at the sight of Ross's gun.

"What . . . what's the meaning of this?"

"We'd like to hear that from you, Manning," Ross said calmly. He put the gun away but, Nella thought, the memory of it in his hand lingered like the Cheshire cat's grin.

"One thing at a time," Buskirk said flatly. "Zaidee says she came in here to see Manning, and got knocked out. Did you do that?"

"I . . . of course not!" Manning sputtered. "She was lying there when I came in."

Buskirk said, "Karate punch, I'd say—here, with the flat of the hand. She's going to have quite a bruise tomorrow."

"Did you see the person?" Ross asked her.

"No. I was just thinking, 'was that a noise?' and I didn't have time to turn around before it—he—hit, and I just went out. It hurts now," Zaidee said in surprise.

"In that location it's just soreness as opposed to anything broken, I would think," Ross said. "You're probably going to need a heating pad on it when you get home. Now, can you remember, was the light on or off as you entered?"

"Off, for sure," she said more steadily. "I reached for the light with my right hand, opening the door with my left. When I saw all this clutter on the floor, I stood in the doorway for a minute or two. I was trying to imagine how it could have happened, like maybe Oscar'd had an epileptic fit or something, but I couldn't see how—"

"I am bleeding," Manning announced with some satisfaction. He had just wiped the hair back from his forehead and seen the blood on his hand. "Surely we can discuss this petty thief, or whatever it is, after I have received medical attention?"

Ross looked at the cut on Manning's temple. "Able's got a first-aid kit upstairs," he said. "Let's adjourn to the ground floor for now. Bill, will you stay here? Send you a replacement as soon as I can. The girls here will take care of your sister."

"Nella, don't let her leave till I've seen her again," Bill cautioned. She nodded, putting an arm around Zaidee. Lottie took the other side with surprising gentleness.

Upstairs, they sorted themselves out. Sergeant Able attended to the cut on Manning's head, both of them sitting on the sofa to one side of Lyle's office. In the big leather chair with Nella nearby, Zaidee didn't mind being questioned by Ross.

"Why did you go to see Manning today, Miss Buskirk?"

"I was going to ask him about a job that's coming up."

"Tell me again how the office looked when you first turned on the light."

She described it again. He went over details: the two piles of papers, the smaller one trailing off toward the closet. Was the closet door open or closed? Open. Light in the closet? Zaidee didn't know. Why had she gone into the room, once she had seen its condition, and that nobody was there?

"I really don't know," she said. "Instinct, I guess. I was thinking how mad Oscar'd be, finding such a mess. I guess I thought I could at least pick up the smaller batch of papers. I just don't know."

"And the next thing you knew . . ."

"Lights out," said Zaidee, wincing.

"Did Manning hit you, Miss Buskirk?"

"Oscar!" The word came out on a crow of laughter, as Zaidee faced the startling picture of Manning as attacker. "Oh, I'm sure he didn't. It must have been—

don't you think—some thief who slipped in by the backstage door?"

"Odd that a thief should just coincide with a murder investigation," Ross said thoughtfully. "Be quite a crime wave for one orchestra within a single week."

"There are such things as anti-libel and slander laws," Manning said menacingly. "I will not sit here and be accused of attacking women in my own office, Lieutenant Ross."

Ross said coolly, "I'll get to you soon, Manning." And to Zaidee again, "Now, as near as you know, what time was it when you entered that office?"

"Well, rehearsal was over at twelve, exactly. I didn't stop for anything but to put my violin in its case . . . my violin!" Zaidee started up.

"I've got it," said Lottie complacently. "It was lying on the floor by you, down there. You must've had it in your right hand, by the handle, and just pushed the light on with your index finger when you went in."

"That's right. That's what happened. Oh, Lottie, thanks . . . I'm so used to carrying it," Zaidee explained to Ross, "I forgot to mention it was in my hand."

"All right. Say it took you five minutes to get down there and get konked. Fair enough? Now, Miss Williams, when did you show up? And what did you do right after rehearsal, so that the two of you didn't see each other on the way?"

"I had a cup of coffee right after rehearsal with Angel Angelo," said Lottie. "It's hard to say how much time that took. The coffee's instant, and self-service up in the lounge, but Angel talks a lot."

Angel talks a lot! Nella looked to see if there was an ironic smile on Lottie's face, but there wasn't. She was dead serious.

"Well, let's figure it backwards," Ross said. "When

you came upstairs and called us, it was just about twelve-twenty, give or take two or three minutes. Say it took you five minutes to notice the scene, shove Manning into the closet, lock it, run up the stairs, and get us back down there . . ."

He broke off to study the dynamic interchange of glances that was going on between Lottie and Manning. As Ross had said, "shove Manning into the closet," Lottie had turned a horrified look on the executive secretary. He had glared back with growing comprehension and fury.

"So that's what happened!" Manning snarled.

Lottie paled. "I couldn't help it!" she gasped. "There was Zaidee on the floor and I couldn't tell who it was bending over her, I thought you—it, I mean—was going to kill her, or make sure she was already dead! Naturally, I thought it was the murderer!"

Strangely, it was evident that Manning's mind took a leap in another direction at this point. Instead of continuing to be furious, he suddenly looked queasy and abstracted, though he kept up his complaint, almost out of a sense of duty.

"Thought I was the murderer! Man goes into his office, his own office, finds some crook has torn it to pieces, finds a body lying in the middle of his floor—and then some imbecilic woman comes along and decides he's a murderer!"

Ross intervened. "Is that what happened, Manning? You came along between the time Miss Buskirk was knocked out and the time Miss Williams came along?"

"Suppose so. I must have," Manning muttered.

"What were you doing when Miss Williams came in? She said you were crouching over the body."

"Of course I was! Had to see if she was alive, didn't I? I was trying to find her pulse; never can find the damn thing in other people. But she was warm, and I saw she was breathing. I was just going to straighten up when this female hit me." He glared at Lottie again.

Having decided by now to take a high moral tone, Lottie gave a sniff and didn't deign to answer.

"Why didn't you let us know, the minute you heard our voices, that you were in the closet?" Ross asked.

"I was knocked out, myself," Manning said. "When I was shoved into the closet, I hit my head on a metal file box that was sticking out on a shelf in there. That's what this cut is." He pointed to Able's neat bandage. "Soon as I came to and realized people were out there, I started banging on the door and yelling."

Sergeant Able had left by now. Bill Buskirk came in, and stood by Zaidee.

"Everything's under way down there, Lieutenant," he told Ross. "Crew's working on it. Able will stay with it. Do you think it's all right if I take my sister home now?"

"I'm fine now, Bill, and I have my car," Zaidee protested.

"So you can drive it, and I'll be right behind you in mine," he said. To Ross he added, "I can be back in thirty minutes, sir. Just need long enough to see her tucked in."

Ross said, "Good idea. Go ahead, Bill. Take your time, but report back here when you're through. This probably is going to take a while."

"I'll call you later," Zaidee said to Nella as she went out with her. "Lottie, thanks again, especially for rescuing this." She held up her violin case.

Lottie stood up, looking anxiously at Ross. "All right if I go, too?" she asked. "I've a million things to do this afternoon."

Ross nodded to the three women. "That's right, all you ladies go on, if you want. I might have a few more questions later. See you tomorrow—you do rehearse on

144

Saturday, don't you?"

"Every day except Wednesday and Monday, and sometimes Sunday, most weeks," Manning said. "We did rehearse last Wednesday morning, but that was an exception. Well, I'll have to be going along, too."

"Not for a little while yet, please, Manning. It'll save time in the long run if you'll stick around now and help us figure out if anything's gone from your office."

Hurrying past Regal McCord's cubbyhole on the way out, Nella gave him a quick wave. She would have liked to have shown him there were no hard feelings about his "joke" the other day, and also about his gossip; but apparently he was still sulky, for he didn't respond, not even to ask her anything about what had happened below.

She would have been more surprised if she had stayed to watch Regal's movements for the next few minutes. Leaving the other hands to complete the buttoning-up process that always followed a rehearsal or a performance, he headed for the backstage double phone booth that Lottie had eavesdropped in before.

This time Regal was more cautious. Using a penknife on his keyring, he poked a small hole in the black plastic patch that covered the hole between booths. While he talked and listened, he applied an eye to the hole from time to time to make sure he was not being monitored.

He got a minion on the first try. Apparently it took some argument to convince her to fetch the party he wanted to the phone. Finally he was talking to the right one.

". . . happens to be urgent, dammit. I know the party's there. Oh, yes, they'll take the call. You just go on, Missy, and announce the name I told you. Hell, yes, they'll take it! So go on and interrupt them!"

At last the right person answered. "What in hell do you mean by calling me here and giving your name?"

Regal's tone was anything but submissive. "You wasn't down there this morning like I told you to be," he grated.

"That's correct. I don't take orders to meet you anywhere, and I don't want phone calls from you—here or anywhere else. You'll be very fortunate if I don't decide to get your job for this insolence."

"Get my job? Let's talk about my job . . . fella can see and hear some mighty peculiar things, doin' the sort of work I do. Find some mighty peculiar things, too."

"What in the hell are you talking about? Don't take that nasty, sly tone with me. What do you mean by it?"

"What if I was to tell you I've got what you're looking for? What you went and messed up Manning's office searching for? And that was a fool idea, by the way. How'd you know you didn't kill that fiddle player, bashing her like that? Lissen, you're gonna pull dumb stunts like that, I don't know if we can do business or not. I don't like dealing with crazy people."

"I don't know what you're talking about." Cold as it was, somehow the voice was not as convincing as the speaker had meant it to be.

Regal's confidence swelled. "You know what I mean, all right. Be damn lucky for you if I don't let Ross know what I mean, too. So when and where can I see you tomorrow—with the cash?"

"If we meet tomorrow, it'll just be a preliminary. I have to see proof; definite proof, or no deal."

"No preliminaries! You be down there tomorrow—tomorrow morning, and I mean early—with the cash!" Regal yelled.

As Regal's voice rose in fury, the other one became calmer and more contemptuous. "Keep your voice down, fool. They can hear you yelling on this end of the line. What time do you arrive in the mornings?"

They set a time and a place. "Bring the cash!" Regal yelled again before he realized that the line had gone dead.

CHAPTER XIV

Manning, left facing Ross alone when the women went home, had some trouble finding answers. Again and again Ross quizzed him on the timing of the events from the end of rehearsal to the scene in his office. Where had Manning been right before he entered his office?

"As a matter of fact, I was in the lounge. I was having a cup of coffee with one of our most important patrons," Manning told him.

"Who was . . . ?"

"Mrs. Nina Oldenberg."

"What was she doing in the hall? You have regular Symphony League meeting times, don't you? Was this one of them?"

"No, Lieutenant. She is talking about setting up a memorial of some kind for Milton Schring—I don't know just what—anyway, Sample, the timpanist, talked to her after a while. When he came along, I headed downstairs for my office."

"And found it torn up, and Zaidee unconscious on the floor."

"That's right."

"I noticed a telephone on your desk down there, Manning. Doesn't it have an intercom set-up? I mean, couldn't you have phoned to, say, this office here, and let someone know there was an unconscious woman down there who needed help?"

"There wasn't time! I'd no more than walked in. The overhead light isn't all that bright, and I didn't stop to light the desk lamp. I had to get down on the floor by her, to make sure she was breathing. When that woman came in and shoved me, I was off balance from leaning over like that.''

Ross switched his field. ''Mr. Manning, who do you think burglarized your office? And what do you think that person was after?''

''Security in this building is non-existent,'' snapped Manning. ''I've told you that from the beginning, Lieutenant. Some sneak thief got in and went through the first place he came to, I suppose. Probably looking for cash; some people keep cash in their desks.'' He shifted uneasily in his chair. His fingers twitched along the edge of his bandage and nervously patted his already combed hair.

''When we talked about the building's security before,'' Lieutenant Ross said in mild surprise, ''you seemed to think it unlikely that a thief would spend his time trying to find something to steal in this building. And if one did, I wonder why he would choose to go down a flight of stairs to raid an office when there's one available on this floor, and some other interesting cubbyholes he could have tried.''

''I can't explain a sneak thief's psychology to you,'' Manning snarled. He was perspiring more than the temperature, which was comfortably cool, seemed to warrant. There was no posing to him now, unless his attempt at heavy sarcasm should be called a pose.

''What's going on here?'' Robert Z. Lyle frowned in the doorway. That was the worst part about using another man's office, thought Ross. You can't throw him out of it, or make too much fuss if he comes in without warning.

''Mr. Lyle. Did you just come into the building?'' Ross asked, pulling his note pad before him.

''No, I've been here awhile. Why?''

"Manning's office downstairs has been burglarized. Papers strewn everywhere. Obviously somebody searching for something. Didn't anybody tell you?"

Lyle said with dignity, "As a matter of fact, I have not been here very long. I have been conferring with a patron. Mrs. Nina Oldenberg. Normally, I would have requested the use of my office for such an interview, but as Mrs. Oldenberg was already in the lounge, we stayed there. She's just left."

"Ah, I see. And where were you before you found Mrs. Oldenberg in the lounge?" Ross made some rapid notes on his pad.

Lyle's silver brows drew together again. "See here, Ross. I've told you before, I don't favor these inquisitions. If you find it absolutely necessary to question my movements, I will arrange a private interview for you as soon as I can find the time."

"I'll count on that." No use, Ross thought, antagonizing the man by questioning him in front of the hired help. "Now, I'm sure you want to learn what has just happened, particularly as one of the musicians was knocked unconscious."

"One of the musicians! Which one?"

"Miss Zaidee Buskirk. But she's quite all right, apparently." Seeing Lyle struggling for identification of a face to match that name, he added kindly, "She's the one whose brother is on my staff."

"Oh, yes . . . violin player, isn't she? Quite all right, you say? Who found her?"

"Manning did. She was lying there, knocked out, papers all over the floor. Apparently she walked in before the burglar had quite finished, so he hid and then zapped her and finished his search."

"Ah. And so you gave the alarm," Lyle said, directly addressing Manning for the first time.

"Well, no," Manning muttered.

150

Ross explained, "Miss Lottie Williams happened to come in while Manning was just checking Miss Buskirk's breathing. She—Miss Williams—took him for the burglar, or perhaps the murderer. She shoved him into the closet, knocking him out in the process. He only came to later, after we had entered the scene."

For a moment, Ross thought Lyle was violently suppressing a cough or a mighty sneeze. Then as he watched, the truth dawned on him. Lyle was struggling not to laugh.

Seizing the opportunity to ease the man out, Ross stepped out into the hallway with Lyle, who had now recovered his composure. "I'll be completely finished with your office soon, I hope, Mr. Lyle," he said. "There's just a bit more checking to be done here, and then we should be able to handle the rest from downtown."

"Quite all right. Take your time," Lyle said graciously. The incident of Manning's having been locked in the closet seemed to have made his day.

Returning to Manning, Ross found him nursing his head in his hands, more sullen than before. "I want to speak to you confidentially, Manning," Ross began.

"Speak away." He didn't look up or move his head from his hands."

"Is your cut really paining you? I'm sorry you were hurt like that."

"Oh, hell no, it feels wonderful." He made it sound as if the whole episode had been Ross's fault alone.

"Try to bear in mind that it was an accident. Miss Williams did what amounts to a brave action. She thought she had captured a murderer. It wasn't her fault that you got in the way, so to speak. Try to remember that."

"Okay, so I remember it. So what?"

"So I'd like to prevent something worse from hap-

151

pening to you."

This got a response. Manning gave him a malevolent, round-eyed stare. "I don't know what you're getting at."

"Then try listening. Has it occurred to you, Manning, that Milton Schring's death might have been an accident?"

"Accident! That's what Lyle tried to tell you the first day, and you wouldn't buy it. So now you've changed your mind!"

"Not at all. I am quite sure that a murderer caused the death of Milton Schring. What I don't know is that he intended Schring to be the victim."

"Of course he was the chosen victim! Why else would the killer have sent him a note?"

"There was no name on that note. What if it had been meant for somebody else? For instance, you?"

A kind of palsy seemed to take Manning's head and hands for a moment. He seemed to quiver like a plucked string. When it passed, however, his manner was as sneering as before.

"Beautiful! You can't solve the murder you've got, just decide it's the wrong victim. Makes it all simple. Choose another one. Anybody'll do—pick on Manning, why don't you?"

"I'm doing my best to warn you that your life may be in danger," Ross said coldly.

"Idiocy! Sheer idiocy! They wouldn't dare," Manning said.

"Who are 'they'?"

"Why . . . any of 'em. Oh, hell yes, some of these little pipsqueaks hate me," Manning went on, his voice gathering force as he spoke. "They know what I can do to them. But there's nothing they can do about it. Nothing they'd dare do. Don't worry about me, Lieutenant," he said on a wave of confidence. "They know better than to try anything with me."

"Very well, Manning. That was all I wanted to say," Ross said abruptly, soothing his own conscience with the inward admonition that it was better to get rid of the man than to hit him.

Waiting a minute to make sure Manning cleared the area, Ross stepped to the office door again. Instead of turning instinctively toward the light at his right hand, he turned to the left. The huge harp case stood only six or eight feet away. Down the hall beyond it, he saw Sergeant Able approaching quietly.

As Ross opened his mouth to speak, Able raised a silencing hand, indicating the far end of the harp case. A couple of steps more brought him to the spot and out of Ross's line of vision. There was a momentary scuffle and an indignant shout.

"Hey! Lemme go! Watcha doing, you . . . !"

Able stepped back into view, holding a writhing Regal by the khaki collar of his work shirt. His face was red with anger.

"An unseen audience, Lieutenant," Able said to Ross. "Wonder how much he managed to overhear?"

"Bring him in and we'll see," Ross said grimly.

Plumping Regal into the leather chair, Able pulled up the straight-backed one close to him. Ross sat in the desk chair. Both policemen stared at McCord. For several minutes, nobody spoke.

Finally Regal snarled, "What in the hell is this all about? Yanking a man away from his work! I'm gonna see that Mr. Lyle hears about this!"

Ross said comfortably, "That may be the best plan, McCord. I was thinking of keeping this interview confidential, depending on whether or not we have your entire cooperation, of course, but you may be right. We may need to consult Mr. Lyle."

McCord's little eyes flickered. "You're bluffing. All I

153

gotta do is tell him how I was getting ready to move that harp case, find a better location for it, and here comes this overgrown bully and hassles me."

Ross said, "While you're telling all that to Lyle, don't forget to explain to him all about that forgery incident that Mrs. Smallwood hushed up for you a few years ago."

All the red drained out of McCord's face as suddenly as it had come. When he managed to speak again, he said almost in a whisper, "What do you want?"

"First, why were you listening behind the harp case?"

Regal decided to try whining. "I'm scared, see? We've got a murderer running loose, haven't we? Naturally I wanted to know what was going on. Who wouldn't? A man's got a right to protect himself."

Ross snapped, "You want to protect yourself? The best way to do that is to start telling the truth. If you have been snooping around, eavesdropping, and have heard something we need to know, or seen something we need to know, now's your chance to tell it. We'll take it from there."

Regal shook his head so that the limp, straw-colored strands of hair stirred about him. "Dunno what you're talking about. Murderers runnin' around loose, all you can think of to do is hassle a man who's tryin' to get his job done. I don't know nothing about it."

They tried for a while longer, but McCord insisted: he didn't know nothing; he hadn't heard nothing; he didn't mean nothing by eavesdropping behind the harp case.

Exasperated, Ross finally said, "Get out of here. And don't let me find you snooping again."

When he had gone, Ross remembered that McCord still had not produced the list of hook users. He told Able, "Try again first thing in the morning to get that list from McCord."

Once at home, Nella found she wasn't able to organize her thoughts and plan how to use her time off. Finally, giving in to exhaustion, she lay down for a nap. It was two hours later that the phone rang.

"How'd you like to go to dinner with the best horn player in Wagner County?" Ralph wanted to know.

"Oh, Ralph, I'm too distracted to go anywhere tonight! Did you hear what's happened?"

"My God, what now?"

She poured out the whole thing to him, feeling immensely better for his sympathetic ear. He was shocked, startled, surprised, and everything she wanted him to be, all in the right order; even amused, finally, over the thought of Lottie's locking Manning into his own closet.

"But you know, Ralph, it really was brave of her. She ought to be appreciated for it. And I'm afraid Manning will take some petty revenge, instead."

"Oh, I doubt if he'll do that. Make him look too silly, don't you think? The best thing for Oscar Manning would be if everybody forgot all about this episode as soon as possible."

"Well, there's comfort in that idea. But why do you suppose someone tore up his office like that?"

"Looking for something, I guess. Something written or typed. Like a memo, or a list, or a letter. Or anything else you could expect to hide in a desk drawer.

"Zaidee must have interrupted him, so he hid nearby, konked her, and finished the search. Cool customer."

"You think it's the murderer."

"What else? It's too much to believe there are two sets of things going on down there, isn't it?"

"Ralph, do you think it's someone crazy? I mean, one of us, supposed to be normal, but really—crazy?"

"A concealed psycho? Certainly not! Now, don't start getting yourself all spooked up, or I'll come over

155

there and drag you out anyway, tired or not. Now look: a mad killer's a mad killer all the time, right? So why would a mad killer kill one time—and plan it all out in advance, don't forget—and then the next time, when it was easier and he had more privacy to kill, simply knock Zaidee out? Answer: because he isn't really a mad killer at all.

"I'm not saying he's smart. That whole booby-trap idea struck me as the work of a criminal fool. But I do think he—or she—is someone who only kills when there's no alternative."

"You're such a comfort. I'm really glad you called me, Ralph."

"Sure you won't go out? Then promise me that you'll have a nice hot bath and get to bed early. Give the shock a chance to wear off. Promise? Good. I'll see you tomorrow."

The telephone rang twice more during the evening. First there was Angel, complaining that she always missed everything, and nobody ever told her anything, so what was going on? Nella suspected that Lottie had given Angel a thorough filling-in already, and that Angel was, in effect, just seeking a second opinion in calling Nella—an instant replay.

Glad of a chance to praise Lottie to her friend, Nella said, "She was really brave, Angel. I'm sure I couldn't have done it. Imagine putting your hand on a murderer's back and shoving him into a closet and locking him in!"

Angel was slightly confused. "But I thought it was Oscar. Didn't you say it was Oscar? I mean, is he the . . . ?"

"Oh, it wasn't really the murderer, but Lottie didn't know that! She *thought* it was."

"Oh." There was a thoughtful pause while Angel attempted to sort it out. Finally she ended the conversation with her own catch-all clause: "Well, I'll ask Ronnie about that."

Zaidee was the other caller. She told Nella that she was in bed with a hot pad on her neck. "Bill is solid mother hen when it comes to my health, you know. He insisted that we stop by the emergency room at Hope Memorial. They took a couple of X-rays, so now he's finally satisfied that I'll survive."

He was due to come back and check on her soon. Yes, she was over the shock now. What did Nella make of the whole episode?

Nella told her Ralph's reason for thinking the killer—if indeed it had been the killer in Manning's office today—was quite sane, and not some member of the orchestra who was an undetected mental case. She was surprised to find that Zaidee wasn't much comforted by this viewpoint.

"But at least, Zee, it's good to know it's a *sane* person," she said.

"Why, particularly? If he kills you, what difference does it make to you whether he's a certifiable nut or not?"

It was an uncomfortable question, for which Nella could find no answer.

CHAPTER XV

Nella found ice on the wooden stairs outside her apartment next morning, and frost on the grass. She had music to return to the basement library in the concert hall and was getting downtown early for the purpose.

Backstage was deserted. A strong coffee aroma permeated the whole area back of stage right. Nella found Regal's hot plate and a coffee pot, loaded but never perked. She turned on the hot plate and headed down the nearby stairs, a bundle of music under her arm.

There were stairs leading to the basement rooms at either end of the horseshoe-shaped backstage. The music library was two flights down at the center of the curve, so it made little difference which stairs one used; the distance was the same.

An incredibly long way, Nella thought, as her footsteps echoed in the hall, past dark, open doorways into unlighted prop rooms, janitors' storerooms, sinister-looking, unidentifiable cubbyholes.

Old Pritchett, the librarian, guarded the music library and its contents. Nella had been told that he had been a trombonist in the orchestra until the librarian's job had been made full-time. That must have been a good twenty years ago, she thought. Now, in his deaf old age, his whole life was tied up in the printed music, and he hated to let any of it out of his sight.

A musician wanting to take home a difficult part had to argue Pritchett out of it, and then sign his life away to get it. Woe unto the player who didn't return the music when it was due!

Nobody knew when Pritchett arrived for work, or when he left in the evenings; he was always there, and the basement halls were always dimly lighted. Even Pritchett's going to look good to me, Nella thought, after these gloomy tunnels. The blank walls were all right; it was the black doorways that were spooky to pass.

Keeping carefully to the middle of the hall, she tried not to speed up going past the next one; it was too childish to be frightened of passing a doorway. She was past it, and going on, before she realized there was something in the room.

That room had not been totally black. Something there had made a sheen; a dull, rectangular kind of background for boots. No, *a* boot. Lying horizontal, three feet or so above the floor, toe up, extending into . . . wrinkles; khakis or Levis? Work pants of some kind to the edge of the sheen, then blackness.

Sometime during the long, long minute that she took to think of all this, Nella had come to a stop. You've got to take a grip on yourself, she told herself. She was an adult; a symphony musician, a responsible member of the community. She must go back and find the light switch and see what was in that room. Let it be a prop, she breathed, something for a Western play, maybe *Oklahoma!* or . . . her hand found the switch and flipped it.

Regal, his face too hideous to know, but his thin yellow hair unmistakeable, now hanging limply from his head at the other end of the short sofa where he sprawled. The one leg she had seen extended over the sofa's other arm, foot posed against some kind of painted screen.

Afterwards, she didn't know how she had gotten from there to the library. Pritchett told her she'd run in screaming and incoherent. It was he who had telephoned for Ross and made Nella sit down on the library's one dilapidated sofa. He had even brought her a cup of water, but her shaking hand had slopped it onto the cherished library carpet, and Pritchett had taken it away again, muttering under his breath. She was sitting on the sofa and Ross was questioning her when her mind began to feel as if it were functioning normally again.

Ross, apparently, had had a good night's sleep. He looked refreshed but grim, and his eyes were a hard ice-green. He asked as many questions of Pritchett as he did of Nella.

"How long has the building been open?"

Pritchett had let himself in the backstage door with a key at a little after six. Hadn't seen Regal or anyone else at that time. He'd come directly down here. Pritchett had his own hot plate and instant coffee mix in a small storeroom past the music stacks.

"Now, when you unlocked the door, did that leave it open? Anyone could get in without a key after that?"

"Of course—that's the way we always do. First man here unlocks the door. That's generally me."

"What made you come so early?"

"Don't have to be made—I like to come early," Pritchett growled.

"Didn't you hear any noise in the hall out there?"

Pritchett indicated the hearing aid in his left ear. "Can't hear thunder with this thing turned off. Soon as I get here and I'm through driving, I turn it off till someone comes in. Gives my ears a rest."

"What time is rehearsal this morning, Miss Payne?"

"Nine-thirty—oh!" She started up, seeing by the library clock that it was past that. Ross waved her back onto the sofa.

"Don't worry about the time," he told her. "Lyle has

160

cancelled rehearsals for today, at my request. I'm afraid that's going to make you double up on a Sunday, tomorrow, according to Manning. He appeared to be mighty upset about the schedule, but we could hardly do anything else. Now, what time was it when you came down here?''

"About fifteen minutes before nine. I wanted to be sure to have time to return the music and get back to warm up."

"You didn't pass anybody, going or coming, including on the stairs?"

"Oh, no."

"Have you heard anything, or seen anything, since the last time we talked, that might shed a light on this—this latest happening?" Nella realized, gratefully, that he was choosing words carefully for her sake, to keep down the shock she was just surmounting.

Had she heard anything? Lottie's gossip! She'd barged in that night, but how much was just Lottie-spite, and how much might be worth Ross's hearing? Unable to decide, she wound up by telling him all of it.

Ross wanted to know each exact word, exact times, exact places, till Nella began to tremble with exhaustion.

When finally he let her go, Zaidee took her away, out of the building into blessed sunshine and cool, clear daylight. "Ralph wanted to wait for you," Zaidee said, "but I shooed him away. Told him I'd be better for you."

They walked, Nella never remembered where, and had coffee in some little shop, and walked again, till she began to be tired and much, much calmer. Zaidee hadn't let her say a word about what she had seen, but now she told Nella to speak about it if she wanted to. Nella told her all the impressions she could remember, and cried a little, and felt better. They were sitting on a stone bench in the little park by the public library.

"It's the same way you said about Schring," Nella said. "So much worse because he was somebody you couldn't like, or feel decently sorry for. Only I do, I do, it was so horrible! But you know what I mean, sorry for *Regal*."

Zaidee said quietly, "I've been thinking. I'm glad now he didn't have any family."

"I didn't know that."

"Well, I don't know if his parents are living or not, but he was married once, years ago, and divorced after a very short time, and there weren't any children. I've always thought that's what made him so—nosey, so involved in all the orchestra cliques and disputes. That was all the life he had. And he was just a born gossip. But I'm glad he didn't leave a wife or children to suffer over this."

"What happened upstairs? I mean, how did they tell all of you what had happened?"

"Why, I suppose you'd say it was very neatly handled. Bill and Sergeant Able suddenly appeared at the entrance doors, and then a couple of uniformed men, but they just let all of us mosey around and finally get into our chairs for rehearsal. Then, with us all gathered in one place and quiet, Sergeant Able told us there had been another murder. He said it was Regal, but he didn't give any details; I didn't know how it had happened till you told me.

"Then they handed out paper and pencils again, and took statements as to when everyone had arrived, where they'd gone, and all that. When they last saw Regal, what he had said, you know the kind of thing. I guess they'll have us all in for individual questioning again."

"Zaidee, who's doing all this?"

Zaidee flipped elegant fingers in a helpless gesture of emptiness. "I've gone over it and over it. First I think Freed; then I think he's impossible. He's too soft. Then

162

I think Regal; well, now we know he wasn't the one.

"Then I think Oscar. For a minute I feel sure that's the right answer, and then I know why I feel that way—just because he's the most despicable person in our orbit."

"I know, I know. Until yesterday, I was almost sure it was Manning. But then, why would he tear up his own office?"

"Well, he wouldn't have to have done that to be the murderer. In fact, maybe, if he's the murderer, he's been killing to protect something that's in his office, that somebody else wants."

"But if it's something that could be found among papers, why would he have to kill to protect it? Why couldn't he just take whatever it is and put it in his bank deposit box—maybe rent a special one, under an assumed name?"

"Oh, I don't know! That's enough about it now. Here we have a whole day on our hands, unexpectedly, or what's left of it. We owe it to ourselves to do something unusual with it."

Not wanting to go back to the parking garage for their cars, they settled on the fine arts museum, which was within walking distance. They strolled the familiar rooms after a soup and sandwich lunch in its small restaurant.

It was almost four o'clock when they returned to the concert hall. Ross was the first person they saw backstage.

"Feeling better, Miss Payne?" he asked kindly. She told him she was back to normal.

"I'm sorry I was such a baby," she said.

"Nonsense. Anybody would have been upset. I'm just sorry I didn't have my man on duty so early. This burglary thing threw me off; didn't get the word to him. Believe me, he'll be there next time."

As Ross had promised, an inconspicuous little man in plainclothes became part of Nella's background that afternoon. He was good at his job; she only noticed him a couple of times. She found even those glimpses greatly reassuring.

Billie Jean Jones waylaid Nella on her way out of the building. "Are you really all right? What a horrible shock for you this morning. What a horrible thing!"

"Oh, I'm back to normal, or as much as any of us can be. Billie Jean, what are we going to do about all this?"

"Bilbo and I are trying to get as many members of the orchestra as possible to come by this evening. Of course, some people will have jobs, since this is a Saturday night, but it seems to be a slack one. We need to get a lot of us together and figure out what we're going to do about Milton and Regal."

"Do about them?" For an instant a ghastly sort of vigilante-notion floated in her mind.

"Oh, I mean about their folks, of course. Bilbo found out that Regal's mother is still living. She's in a nursing home up east, but she's fit to travel if she had the money. It wouldn't take much if we all contributed."

"I'll be there, Billie. I'm phone Ralph Payton and see if he'll take Zaidee and me, so that'll be three of us. I'm glad you and Bilbo are working on it. You always seem to be the ones who take care of things like this."

"I guess we ask for it. Overactive parental glands, probably. All right, then, I'll put you down for woodwinds. We're trying to make sure all the sections are represented, and to get quite a few from the fiddles, of course."

On an impulse, Nella asked the same question she had asked Zaidee earlier: "Billie Jean, who do you think is behind all this?"

"I've been giving it a lot of thought," Billie Jean

said, "and of course Bilbo and I have discussed it *ad nauseum*. But all I've really come up with is a feeling. I've got a feeling it isn't somebody really in the orchestra, but a—a hanger-on. Somebody close by."

"Why do you believe it isn't someone in the orchestra?"

"Please don't laugh; well, I know you won't. But look at it this way: musicians spend their whole lives learning to be precise. Isn't that a fact? Hitting the right note, at the right time, with the right degree of force.

"If you look, you see that carry over into other aspects of their lives. Some people have been surprised at how blunt some musicians are in their conversation. It seems as if they'd rather be accurate than tactful. But I don't look at it like that. I think it's just a logical extension of their musical training. To be precise. Well, it seems to me that this crime is the most imprecise thing —series of things—I've ever seen. A booby-trap! Then searching Manning's desk—and getting interrupted at that!"

Nella said, "But strangling Regal, that was precise enough."

"Was it? What if he'd been faster, or stronger, than the murderer calculated? And wasn't the rope just picked up from backstage somewhere? That's what I heard." Seeing Nella shudder, Billie Jean said, "Oh, I'm sorry, I forgot. Anyway, I still feel, somehow, that it's going to be somebody outside the orchestra."

Feeling her spine creep, Nella thought, one of the stagehands. Old Pritchett. Who else? She asked aloud, "Who else?" and Billie Jean must have been on the same wave length.

"Well, I really shouldn't say, but . . . maybe somebody like Nina Oldenberg, for instance."

"Nina Oldenberg! Why, she's a millionaire! She can do anything she wants to, go anywhere, and with all the men in her life, past, present, and future, she's got to be scandal-proof! Why in the world would she need to murder anyone?"

"Oh, I know all that. But you know how she hangs around the orchestra—always backstage, fluttering around. She was all over Trevelyn the other night until Lyle led him away, so I was told. I thought, some time before that, that she was taking an interest in our Milton."

"Now, that I can believe, and vice versa. But they both were notorious for having affairs—you know what everyone said about Milton. And, for Pete's sake, her husband must have lost count years ago! So why would she have to kill him, just because their affair was over?"

"Maybe she didn't want it to be over, and Milton did. And maybe Regal caught on, somehow, and threatened her?" Billie Jean ended on an uncertain note.

Nella shook her head. Beautiful Nina Oldenberg certainly was rich in her own right, but it was hardly possible to picture her deeply caring for any man, let alone a self-centered one like Schring.

"Well, I said it was just a feeling," Billie Jean said. "See you tonight. Anytime after seven."

Getting into her car, Billie Jean was hailed in her turn. She could hardly repress a guilty blush when she saw it was Nina Oldenberg. Covering the feeling, she greeted Nina warmly. "My, you look wonderful!"

It was the simple truth. She was spectacular in soft gray and flamingo pink. The cold wind flirted lovingly with her thick black hair where it lay in shining waves over her shoulders. Her lipstick, exactly matching the flamingo scarf that was tucked into the broad suede collar of her gray coat, looked both theatrical and entirely right.

"Thanks, Billie Jean," she smiled enchantingly. "I've been looking for you inside. Bilbo told me you're assembling all the players you can at your home this evening."

"That's right. We can't get everybody on such short notice, but we think it's important that we get together about Milton's and Regal's families, and so on."

"What does 'and so on' include?" asked Nina rather sharply.

"I'm not sure I know, exactly," Billie Jean said slowly. "But somehow, with these horrible murders going on, we just feel, maybe I should say, I just feel, that it's time to circle the wagons, get together and . . . I don't know. Maybe just reassure each other."

"I feel very much the same way," Nina said. "Would you mind very much if Juley and I came?"

"Why, of course not! We'd be delighted to have you," Billie Jean said.

"We've been fumbling around, wondering how to go about it," Nina explained, "and I think this might be the answer. You see, we want to make a memorial for Milton. A musical one. It seems to me, and I know Juley will agree, that we ought to consult the musicians about it. I've been trying to ask individual ones. The best way to do it, you know. So your meeting will be just made to order for us."

Billie Jean gave her the time and her address and stood for a moment watching as Nina hurried away, looking like a pink and gray flower caught in the wind.

CHAPTER XVI

Long ago the Joneses had invested in a huge coffee urn for their frequent entertainments. It was going full force when Nella arrived with Zaidee and Ralph that evening and walked into a buzz of people in the family room. Billie Jean had set around a few large platters of cookies and snacks, but the meeting was plainly dedicated to somber discussion.

Sample, the timpanist, beamed on the trio from the kitchen doorway. "Good to see you. You all right, Nella? You're looking mighty pretty tonight." She couldn't believe he'd ever growled at anybody in his life.

She felt pretty. She wore a pale orange dress that blended in tone with her coppery hair. It was a blessing to put on light or bright colors after the boring black of concert nights.

It hardly surprised Nella, after what Billie Jean had said that afternoon, to see Nina Oldenberg make an entrance. The same quiet-looking man was in tow; he must be the husband, whose name nobody could remember.

Ralph caught Nella's arm and pulled her off to one side to greet his stand partner, Pete Rollinson. Pete was a beautiful man; willowy, medium-sized, athletic looking. His curly blonde hair completed a picture that was almost too perfect.

When she had first entered the orchestra, Nella had wondered why such a gorgeous hunk was not constantly surrounded by women. Sometime during the first week she had discovered the answer. Pete was a homosexual and proud of it. After the initial surprise, Nella had made a further interesting discovery: that it didn't make any difference to her. She liked him and enjoyed his company.

"I wanted to be with you today," Ralph said to her, "but I thought Zee had a better idea. You all right?"

"Oh, yes, I'm back to normal," Nella said. "Zee and I walked and talked till the shock wore off. But I'm glad not to be home alone tonight. I guess all of us feel that way. It's like Billie Jean and Bilbo to think of this. Even if we don't accomplish anything, we can give each other moral support."

Pete smiled and patted her arm. "Good girl. We'll have to keep a better eye on you after this."

For a moment Nina Oldenberg had dropped onto the arm of the big chair where Angel was sitting. They made an enchanting contrast. Nina was well-curved and enticing in a dress that had great splashes of red and yellow on a dark background that complemented her glossy black hair. Angel, in pale yellow, was wispy and fragile.

Other people settled onto chairs and sofas and the carpet as Bilbo took the floor. He explained that Regal's mother had been anxious to come when he had suggested that the musicians might finance her trip. "The round-trip ticket on the plane and her hotel bill and meals for a couple of days will come to less than four hundred dollars," he said. "She can't stay in Regal's apartment; he was sharing it with a fellow who works nights. If everyone could put in five dollars, we'd have plenty and enough left over to send a nice wreath to the funeral and hand the rest to her for taxis and incidentals."

When people began murmuring assent, Bilbo asked

four guests in different areas of the room to begin collecting. From a list of Symphony personnel, he ticked off names of absent players to be contacted later. Someone volunteered to meet Mrs. McCord's plane; someone else, to return her to the airport when she was ready to go.

Marcus Belle asked, "How's Millie Schring doing? Is she all right, financially?"

"She's in good shape for money," Billie Jean said. "Milton left her a large insurance policy, and she intends to go back to work right away. His funeral expenses, and Regal's too, for that matter, are paid for by their insurance."

"Well, then," Belle summed up, "both sets of expenses are pretty well taken care of. Millie's daughters are with her right now. What else can we do for her?"

"The main thing I thought of is the instruments," Bilbo said. "I don't think Millie or her folks know anything about clarinets or any kind of musical equipment, and you know Milton has several very valuable instruments at home. Billie and I thought maybe someone who knows about saxes and clarinets could . . ."

"I have his B-flat clarinet now. I told Millie I'd be glad to go see what he has, and try to evaluate the things," Nella said. "But to tell you the truth, I think Freed has a lot more experience and would be a lot better judge than I am."

"Oh—Freed!" Lottie hissed. "Don't bring his name into it. How do we know he's not responsible for all this trouble, himself?"

Horrified, most of the hearers glanced hurriedly around to see if Freed was there. He was not.

In the shocked silence that fell, Nella heard a deep-drawn breath beside her, where Pete Rollinson stood. Turning, she was surprised to find that his face was darkly flushed. His voice, unfortunately high-pitched, quivered with anger as he answered.

"*Miss* Williams," he snapped, "that remark was not just in bad taste. It was unforgivably irresponsible. I demand that you either provide evidence to back up that accusation, or withdraw it, at once."

Nella felt like applauding, though the effect was a little marred by Pete's girlish toss of the head at the end of his speech.

"Well, I *must* say!" Lottie glanced around her for support and met with rigid stares that told her she had gone too far.

Billie Jean said half-heartedly, "Oh, now Pete . . ."

"No, dear," he said tensely. "This is serious. No one has the right to make that kind of accusation in a public gathering like this, without offering evidence to back it up." He glared at Lottie. "I'm waiting."

Lottie flapped a helpless hand in his direction. "Well, it was just a passing remark, sort of a joke, you might say. Well, I never thought it'd be taken so seriously . . ." As she trailed off, everybody else began talking at once, and the moment of friction passed.

Billie Jean called for order again. "We are pleased to have a special couple with us tonight," she said. "They are well-known to all of you in the orchestra. May I present two of our most faithful Symphony sponsors, Mr. and Mrs. Julius Oldenberg."

"Call me Nina," invited Nina Oldenberg with a wide, easy model's smile, "and this is Julius. We are very sorry to intrude upon you in a time of grief like this, but Juley and I need your help.

"We were especially fond of Milton Schring, and thought the world of him—as a musician—didn't we, Juley? So we want to make a fund, an endowment arrangement, with one of the universities close by, and designate it as something like, 'The Milton Schring

171

Scholarship,' or something like that.

"We want you people to help us decide which university, and what sort of rules to set up for using the funds, and so on. Should it be just for clarinet players, or for all woodwinds, or . . . ?"

"Strings are the basic orchestral instruments," remarked one of the viola players.

"Don't forget the percussion," boomed Sample.

Angel said, "If you open it to all sorts of instruments, how could you exclude, for example, the marching band people? Pretty soon you might be awarding scholarships to people who could never even get into a major orchestra."

"Wait, wait, wait!" Bilbo rapped a pencil against a glass till the room quieted. "I suggest we elect a committee of not more than, say, six players to help the Oldenbergs set up their endowment. Could we see a show of hands, for or against setting up a committee of six? Thank you—it looks almost unanimous. Let's have your nominations, please."

Quickly the group selected six players, including Bilbo, Ralph Payton, and Toby Whitemore. Feeling a pang of uneasiness, Nella realized she didn't relish the picture of Ralph's meeting with the glamorous Nina, alone in her palatial home.

The six committee members were asked to adjourn for an initial meeting with the Oldenbergs in the Joneses' studio across the hall. Billie Jean moved about, urging snacks and coffee on the remaining guests.

Nella drifted over to a corner where Toby and Evvie, hand-in-hand but both wearing thundercloud expressions, were converging on Pete. She said lightly, "Congratulations on your committee appointment, Toby."

Evvie sniffed. "I don't see what's so wonderful about it," she said. "Getting stuck on a committee with that

172

grabby nymphomaniac. Just watch—she'll drag the thing on and drag it on, until it becomes a permanent arrangement.''

"Be a little awkward for her to get romantic, don't you think?'' Pete asked mildly. "What with a six-member committee, and half of them female.''

"Oh, she'll find a way,'' Evvie went on snappishly. "Telephone calls at odd hours, say, and could he please drop by and pick up this special letter, or report, or some such thing. Ralph, too, I wouldn't wonder,'' she added, turning on Nella. "Don't tell me *you* like this idea!''

Nella was more embarrassed than she intended to show. She said airily, "Oh, Ralph isn't my property to worry about, you know. Cheer up, Evvie, it's not the end of the world.''

Toby was attempting to disengage his hand without being obvious about it. "Well, so long,'' he said, "guess I need to get on in there for the meeting.''

Evvie latched on tighter, pulling him toward the kitchen. "You promised to fix me a drink first, Toby. You know just the way I like them. Come *on*. We brought along some bourbon,'' she added to the others as they walked away.

"People!'' Pete muttered. "What makes them act the way they do? Crazy, half the time. Like that crank, Lottie Williams. I hope I didn't snap her up too sharply.''

Nella said, "I didn't know you and Freed were friends.''

"Howard Freed is a really fine person, and a talented man—very, very talented,'' Pete said warmly. "I just won't stand for that silly old bitch gossiping about him, just to get herself some attention.''

"I wonder.''

"You wonder what?''

173

"Why, if Lottie really is throwing all those accusations around just to get attention," Nella said slowly. "I hadn't thought much about it till tonight—but she runs almost too true to form, doesn't she? Could she have some other reason for wanting to pin the murder on somebody?"

"Like self-defense, you mean? I wouldn't mind thinking so! But what earthly reason would Lottie have for getting rid of Schring? Because if Regal knew who had committed the first murder, then that supplies the motive for killing him, but not everybody had a motive for murdering Schring."

Or Manning, thought Nella—if indeed his coat had gotten mixed up with Milton's and the note had been put into the wrong pocket. Except for the general dislike of the whole body of musicians, what would be a motive for putting Manning out of the way?

He had come in, she saw, just in time for the voting. Now he advanced on their corner, his face expressing noble suffering and dignified regret for the passing of old friends. A smaller bandage now covered the cut on his temple.

"Hello, Oscar," they said in unison.

"Nella . . . Pete. A sad occasion—a very sad occasion. One never knows, in this life, does one? Poor Milton—a dedicated artist, taken away from us in the prime of life. Makes you wonder, doesn't it?"

Pete remarked wickedly, "That's just what Nella was doing. Wondering."

Oscar Manning's paternal beam all but patted Nella on the head. "What was our little Nell wondering about?"

"Oh just . . . why all this had to happen," Nella mumbled. She shot Pete an "I'll see you later" glance.

Manning had no doubts. He had pondered this disturbing situation, and had come to a conclusion that fit in with his sense of values. Therefore, it must be the answer. "Why, I think Lottie Williams may have put her finger on the answer the other day—inadvertently, of course. She suggested, you remember, that Regal must have been playing a bad joke, or meaning just to frighten Schring, and that he had gone too far."

Pete looked grim, but he didn't speak of Lottie's new outburst a few minutes ago.

In simple astonishment, Nella asked, "But then—who do you think killed Regal?"

Manning rode triumphantly to a conclusion on the crest of coincidence. "Very likely some outsider. Unfortunately, the building is open before dawn, with old Pritchett getting here so early. All someone with a private grudge would have to do is to slip inside the stage door after Regal, follow him downstairs, and—zing!"

Pete asked uneasily, "How did he . . . wasn't he strangled? From the back? I mean, was there an instrument, a rope, or something?"

Manning said, "It was just a length of ordinary thin rope. They've got it all sizes, all thicknesses, all over the place backstage. Use it for everything."

"But wouldn't it have to be a pretty strong person? At least, someone stronger than Regal himself?" Nella wanted to know. "He must have been in good condition just from doing the kind of work he did. Regal, I mean."

"Not necessarily. Speed would be the difference," Manning said. "Catching him off balance, you see, he's fighting not to fall down before he can worry about what's around his neck. Ross thinks a woman could have done it."

Manning reassembled his condolence-face and hurried away to another group. Pete looked after him speculatively.

"Did you notice there was one thing he left out of his calcuations altogether?" he asked.

"You mean the burglary—if that's what it was? Yes, I kept waiting for him to fit that into his theory. He told the lieutenant from the first that he thought some thief had wandered in and done it. Do you suppose that's his real opinion?"

"Don't you believe it! He knows what the burglar was after. It follows that he knows who the burglar is, doesn't it? And if they're the same person, doesn't he have to know also who the murderer is? Why isn't he telling?"

"I don't see that it follows, necessarily. I mean, that he knows who the murderer is, or believes that he knows. Suppose Oscar really is sure who the burglar is, and what he's after but doesn't believe him to be the same person as the murderer? Or her, of course."

"But that's stupid. No—don't answer that remark; I know what you're thinking. Oscar *is* stupid, or so we like to tell each other. But is he really dumb, Nella? Could he be, and have built up the little empire he has, between managing the orchestra personnel and controlling the luxury jobbing all over town?"

Nella said, "All right. Let's say he's smart, in terms of business and making money. But he's really dumb, or just plain blind, about human relations and motivations. Maybe it's a plain old lack of imagination."

"Maybe he's playing detective? Looking for evidence to turn in along with his ideas?"

"A dangerous game," Nella shook her head. "I wouldn't wish even Oscar that kind of trouble."

Nella strolled off to Bilbo and Billie Jean. She promised them she'd talk with Freed about Schring's instruments at the rehearsal next morning.

As soon as Ralph came back from the committee meeting in the studio, Zaidee and Nella were ready to go. Nina Oldenberg favored him with a special good-bye clasp of the hand.

In the car, Nella asked crossly, "Does she gush like that all the time?"

"The flow is fairly constant," Ralph said. "What is really interesting to watch is old Juley's reaction. Every time she pauses, or says, 'don't we, Juley?' or 'isn't that right, Juley?' he nods. Never answers in words; just nods. He must have grown a hinge in the back of his neck by now."

"Well, that's a pretty cheap price to pay," Zaidee said, "considering the poor guy's so dumb he'd be selling apples on the corner if he hadn't had a rich daddy, and she keeps him up to snuff with all the high-powered socialites in his family's circle."

"Why do you suppose she married him?" Nella asked.

"She likes being married," Zaidee said. "It's hard for a woman like Nina to find just the right sort of man: agreeable, quiet, ready to mind his own business, not jealous, and having a perfectly gorgeous body. He's number four, and seems to be working out better than any of the others. I rather like the guy. He's generous. I'd guess this endowment fund may be his idea."

"It's hard to fault the idea," Ralph said. "And the endowment they're talking about putting up is a mighty nice chunk. We're going to have to do a real job of planning to make sure it's effective and gets to the right students."

At Zaidee's house, they watched her unlock the door and step in before backing out of the drive. Bill's car, which stayed outside the garage when he was home, was not visible.

"Poor Buskirk must be working late on this case again," Ralph remarked. "Do you think they'll start over on all of us in the morning?"

"I don't see what good it'd do," Nella said. "Most people seem to think that Regal was killed because he knew who murdered Schring . . . or said he did.

"You know, that's what's so awful to me. I can just picture poor, dumb Regal, hinting and grinning and pretending to know all about it—and really not knowing a thing! But convincing the killer, who would already be nervous about it, that he had to be gotten rid of."

"I don't see it like that," Ralph said heavily. "I just have a feeling that the killer knew exactly what Regal was like. What all of us are like. Somehow, I think he's a watchful, methodical person. Even with that booby-trap that everybody says was so sloppy, I think maybe he was simply willing to take either consequence: that it would kill, or that it would just serve to scare his victim. I can't see him killing anybody on the basis of hints and grins."

"Makes you feel spooky, doesn't it? The idea that somebody evil is out there, watching us all."

"You and I are outsiders," Nell," Ralph said. "That's what I want you to remember in all of this. We're new here, we don't know these people the way they know each other. Except superficially, we're not involved."

They had just pulled up in front of her apartment building. As Ralph climbed the stairs behind her, Nella sighed, "You always manage to make me feel better."

"When this mess is over, and we get a chance to think about ourselves, I'm thinking about making a career of it."

"Of what?"

"Making you feel better," he grinned.

"Oh." He had taken her key and unlocked the kitchen door, but she held out her hand for it. "No, don't come in tonight. On second thought, come in and look in the closets for me, if you will, but then let's say goodnight. I want to have you come over soon, but not after a day like today."

He came and looked into every closet space big enough to hold a man. Then, in the kitchen, he put his arms around her. "When I kiss you, it's going to be a good one," he said. "Hold onto that thought, please. No, don't come out again. Goodnight."

He was gone, clattering down the stairs. Nella stood exactly where he had held her until she heard his car drive away.

CHAPTER XVII

Talking to Freed was unexpectedly easy, for he arrived for the Sunday morning rehearsal as early as Nella did.

"I'd like to help Mrs. Schring. I'd especially like to, because of the other situation—the audition thing, you know—I'd like to, sort of make amends if she'll let me," Freed said uncomfortably.

"I should think she'd be very grateful," Nella said. "Would you like me to set up an appointment and go along with you to break the ice? I don't know Millie well myself, but at least we've met."

"Oh, yes, I'd appreciate that. And then we could have two opinions about the instruments, too. Suppose I call you next week sometime and set up the times and places."

"Here's my phone number—let me write it for you." She was just handing it over when Ralph came up.

"Giving your phone number to strange men, are you?" he teased her as they moved away.

"Doesn't seem to make you jealous in the least," she smiled.

"Not as long as the men are that strange!"

"Poor Freed; nobody likes him. Come to think about it, though, I believe Pete Rollinson does. He stood up for him at Joneses' last night."

"That's just what I mean," Ralph said. "I think that's the answer to Freed's mysterious behavior, and why he wouldn't tell what he was doing, hanging around last Tuesday night."

"He said he was waiting for Schring, didn't he?"

"Made a good excuse, and Schring couldn't deny it, being dead. You wait for a corpse, you wait a long time. He was really waiting for Pete, if I have him diagnosed correctly—not knowing he'd missed him and Pete had already gone home."

"But why—oh! You think—"

"Exactly. I suspect those two are in the early stages of a romance—and didn't care to let Ross in on it. They could always confess to it, if the police really leaned on them, but until such time, they would probably prefer to keep their romance a secret. Look at the way they took off when we parked next to them after the funeral."

"Maybe that's the reason why I saw both of them, popping in and out of the Mauve Room, and each being noncommittal about why he was there."

"Thursday afternoon? Very likely. Pete has dropped a hint or two lately. Poor guy, there's never anybody he can feel free to discuss his love-life with. His roommate moved out three or four weeks ago, and he's been lonely. You know he never would deliberately try to seduce anybody, but I think Freed gradually let him know he's interested."

"When did he become so secretive? I thought Pete was rather proud of being a homosexual, though he hasn't made any references to it around me."

"Pete's not ashamed of himself, but he's almighty careful not to be offensive to anybody. In this case, I think he's being extra careful because Freed doesn't want anybody knowing about it."

"Oh, dear."

"Well, I don't know. Long as they don't bother anybody. You never even noticed anything gay about Freed, did you? Gay! What a misnomer! Poor old Pete seems to spend three-fourths of his time miserable. I'm always having to cheer him up."

"Freed's no ray of sunshine, either. His conversation during rehearsals ranges from negligible to none. Oh, well, maybe they'll be good for each other. Look, it's time to get onstage."

Derek John, the regular conductor, was back for this unusual Sunday double. Most of the audience liked him, and all of them respected him on an artistic level. Finding his orchestra distracted by two murders and a burglary, however, he had flown into an Olympian rage. This added tension only increased the upset of the musicians. When Marcus Belle asked the oboe for an "A" to tune the orchestra, he rejected the pitch. Instead of tuning his violin to the oboe, he shook his head and gave back an "A" which was just a shade higher.

Color rushed into the oboist's face. Defiantly he sounded the same "A" as before. Belle shook his head again, insisting on the higher note. The first violins chimed in, several of them just a hair higher than the note set by Belle. He, in turn, began to darken with rage.

Hampered by his valuable instrument, the oboist looked around for a vent for his wrath. Finally he snatched the pencil kept on the stand for marking parts, and hurled it across the room. It made such an incongruous little "tick" on landing that somebody laughed.

"Maestro!" the oboist appealed, "if these tin-eared jerks don't want my 'A,' let them tune up each other. Every time I give them the note, they climb the pitch. There's not a bit of use in my sitting here getting insulted by idiots who can't recognize A-440 when they hear it!"

"Now, Mr. Oboe," soothed John, "I'm sure there's nothing personal intended. When people are nervous, they tend to tune a bit sharp. Mr. Belle," he said, laying a soothing hand on Marcus's shoulder, "please. Let's all abide by the oboe's 'A.' That means everyone." He looked meaningfully about at the other strings, all of whom avoided his glance.

Everybody knew his explanation was only part of the answer. As a private teacher had explained it to Nella years ago, "climbing the pitch" is a tricky little game that string players are bad about playing. They know the musician whose instrument is just a tad sharper than those around him will sound brighter, more brilliant. It's a naughty little game that can quickly get out of hand.

During the tuning-up process that now proceeded, Nella found herself looking at the sea of hands all around her. Almost without exception, the hands she could see were well-kept, most often with delicate, slender fingers moving over the instruments with agile grace. Beautiful hands, she thought; skilled, talented fingers. Could it be that one of those pairs of hands in front of her had also skillfully murdered? She forced her mind back to the music.

Nothing pleased Derek John. Again and again the rehearsal was stopped for individual parts to be scrutinized, played, argued over. The small mistakes in reading, the squeaky notes, multiplied as John's scalding sarcasm exacerbated nerves already tingling. For that morning, at least, nobody thought of anything but music. By the noon break, everyone was exhausted.

"Two more hours of the Old Man this afternoon," groaned Zaidee to Nella at the coat hooks. "Don't know if I can stand it."

"You'll stand it," Ralph muttered at her other side. He was waiting to go to lunch with Nella. "It's the horns he hates today."

It was a relief getting out into the fresh air, damp and cold though it was. Nella said, "Let's don't say a word about music for a whole hour."

"Agreed," Ralph said. "Anyway I wanted to ask you

about something else." He turned and looked at her very seriously.

Oh, dear, thought Nella, why didn't I see this one coming? She had in mind her promise to Ross to say nothing about the idea that Schring might have been the wrong victim. If there was any danger at all in knowing of that theory, Ralph was the last person she'd want to share it with. "And not about the murder, either," she amended hastily.

"But I don't get your attitude, Nella," he said earnestly. "I've been hearing some pretty strange comments. People, and I don't mean just Lottie and Angel, seem to believe that you may be holding some information back."

"Oh, this orchestra!" she said. "A hotbed of gossip! What would I know, more than anybody else? Please, Ralph, I just can't stand to think about it any more today. But I do give you my word on this: I don't know anything, not a single thing, that Lieutenant Ross doesn't know. I promise."

As soon as the words were out of her mouth, she remembered that she'd never mentioned Manning's remark about his coat to the policeman. But surely they'd checked into the hooks business thoroughly by now: so what she'd just said was still the literal truth.

Uneasily, Ralph took her at her word. During lunch they talked only about themselves, probing into each other's backgrounds and ideas. For them, it was fascinating enough so that they gradually forgot the worries of the moment.

She learned that Ralph, like herself, had grown up in a small town. For him, too, the preoccupation of his youth was to get to the conservatory.

"My dad is a high school coach," he told her. "Luckily for both of us, he has my brother Evan to make into a football player. That way, he didn't mind so much that I took seriously to music."

"What did your mother think about it?"

"Oh, she was always in favor of my music. It comes from her side of the family, I guess. We lost her a couple of years ago—to cancer."

"I'm sorry."

"One good thing, she said she could die happy, knowing both of us had a good start in what we wanted to do."

By the time they had walked back, they were laughing and chatting over conservatory anecdotes. Nella didn't even notice the inconspicuous little man who followed them to lunch and followed them back to the hall. Ralph, however, did.

When the musicians were assembled to begin the afternoon session, Lyle stepped onto the podium and rapped for attention. Startled faces turned to him from private chats and last-minute warmups.

Those who knew him well enough were startled to see the changes picked out by the bright rehearsal lights. Even his silver hair seemed drained of vitality, lying flatter than usual on his head. He had forgotten, for once, to remove his reading glasses, and they accentuated the tired lines around his eyes. Deep grooves ran from his nose to the corners of his mouth, seeming to tug them downward.

Lyle explained that the Symphony League Board intended to advertise blind auditions for the clarinet solo chair next week. He thanked them for the actions they had planned at the Joneses' and explained what steps the Board was taking toward funeral arrangements for Regal.

Zaidee remarked afterwards, "The Big Man looked pretty sick, didn't he? Why in the world didn't he have Manning tell us all that, in the usual way?"

Bill, who had come to escort his sister home, said,

"Ever occur to you that he may not trust Manning any more? I've been watching. Every time they've been in a room together, he always manages not to say a word directly to Manning. It wouldn't surprise me if he really suspected Manning of the murders."

Manning as the murderer? Nella shuddered. It was easy, so easy to picture Manning sneaking from behind, setting a trap.

As the two of them stepped out the backstage door, Zaidee took her brother by the arm. "Bill, I'm getting scared."

All of Bill Buskirk's protective instincts centered in his small but precious older sister. "Tell me, Zee. Just talking about it might help."

"Well, it's hard to explain. But all day today, when we were sitting there supposedly making music together, we really weren't *together* at all. I mean in harmony, both ways. Oh, I don't want to sound like a bad imitation of the Great Artiste," she said, "but an orchestra is supposed to be an instrument. For the conductor, you know.

"You always claim not to know anything at all about music, but I know you know about that. It's like all the other violins and I are just a small part of a big, big chord. Maybe it takes the whole ensemble to make the complete chord; maybe just a part. But being in on it is a big experience.

"Now this thing comes along; this violence. It's a discord. Like a horrible, jangling, jarring noise in the middle of the piece. It tears up your nerves and destroys the harmony, the blend. I can't bear the idea that one of us has really killed. I'm scared it might happen again. I'm scared I might glance up during a rehearsal or a performance, and suddenly be looking a murderer in the eyes. Most of all, I'm scared of what this situation is doing to our characters."

"For Pete's sake, Zee—what has your character got to do with it?"

"Well, just look at the suspicious way people are looking at each other. We're all snapping each other's heads off. And the gossips! I thought Angel Angelo and Lottie Williams were bad before . . . now, you can't afford to say hello to them! And speaking of Lottie— she's gone downright wacko, accusing first one person and then another of being the murderer. If nothing else, someone's going to wind up suing her for slander."

"Now, perhaps I can ease your mind at least a little about that one," Bill said. "As you say, she's pretty hard to take. In fact, the lieutenant practically runs when he sees her coming. He forced her onto me the last time she came up with another hot tip."

"Whom was she accusing this time?"

"I never found out. I asked myself, 'what's this old gal really up to with all these accusations?' and an idea occurred to me. So I pursued it," said Buskirk smugly.

"How? What did you do?"

"Put on the tough act. Put on the pressure, really hard, about why she was still in the building so late. Remember, or maybe you didn't know the details, but she said she'd been having coffee with Angel. But it seems that Angel had had time to pour her own coffee, cream and sugar it, let it cool, sip it slowly, and still be through ahd ready to go at about the time Lottie was just sitting down with her."

"How in the world do you know all that?"

"Actually, it was just good old police routine." Bill enjoyed nobody's admiration as much as Zaidee's. He beamed. "The details about the coffee were supplied, after a good deal of memory-prodding, by Mr. Julius Oldenberg. It seems he came in after both of them and asked to sit with them while his wife was visiting down-stairs. He'd no sooner got settled in a chair than Angel was up and off, leaving him stuck with Lottie.''

"Yes," mused Zaidee, "that's the sort of thing a man would remember."

"Well, Lottie finally confessed what she hadn't wanted to tell about her movements from right after the concert until she went upstairs for coffee," Bill said. "It seems she'd been suspicious for a long time that Nina Oldenberg was corrupting the morals of one of the musicians.

"It wasn't that Lottie meant to do anything about it; she just wanted the pleasure of knowing other people's secrets and spreading them around. Well, you know what she's like! So she made up her mind to spy on the woman when she noticed her ditching her husband backstage."

"But wait," Zaidee objected. "Did you say her husband went upstairs and joined Lottie and Angel there?"

"Not right then," Bill said. "There was anywhere from a fifteen-minute to a twenty-minute interval. Oldenberg wasn't trying to deceive us," he added. "He said he'd gone to the men's room. Ran into Marcus Belle and they started talking. He doesn't know, to the minute, how long. Then when Marcus took off to go home, Julius went upstairs.

"That gave Lottie some spying time. I take it she did the whole cloak-and-dagger routine, even to hiding behind that damned harp case my men keep tripping over. Finally she got her reward: saw Nina involved in a serious conversation with a man. In fact, Lottie says, it looked more like the beginnings of a fight."

"Which man?"

"Manning. That's what has Lottie so scared she's running around in circles, trying to prove she suspects everybody else. She's terrified that Manning will think she's trying to pin something on him. And then she had

188

to get unlucky and be the one to lock him in his own closet!''

Zaidee laughed. ''I'm not sure how much sense all that makes, but then when did Lottie Williams ever make much sense? You do cheer me up, Little Brother. Whatever would I do without you?''

CHAPTER XVIII

After she said goodbye to the Burkirks, Nella put away her instrument with an unaccustomed feeling of relief. It had been a long, mean day, fighting John's temperament and her own distractions with every measure. Ralph called to her across the empty rehearsal room, "Wait for me, Nell! I'm seeing you home."

It really was too much for one twenty-four hour period, she realized. She definitely should put him off to another time, she thought, as, feeling her face flush with pleased surprise, she nodded. There! Every key was inspected, and the pad she had thought might be loose was in perfect condition. She walked over and waited while Ralph finished talking to Pete.

He followed her little car easily through the light Sunday evening traffic.

"Come in for a drink," she offered when they stood at the foot of her outside stairs.

"Thanks—I hoped you'd ask."

"It's no big invitation. All I have is some Scotch. We can have Scotch and water if that's all right with you."

"The very best. Ah, the books. I wanted to browse when I spotted them last night," Ralph said as they entered the tiny apartment. Through the open kitchen door he had seen the makeshift plank-on-brick bookcases Nella had fashioned to cover one living room wall.

"A gradual accumulation. Don't look for any plan or method about them," she cautioned, putting ice into glasses and measuring whiskey and water. "Would you by any chance be interested in some warmed-over meat-loaf? I broke down and made one the other night, and it'll take me forever to finish it off by myself. If you don't mind leftovers, I could make a salad, and maybe—''

''Accepted, say no more! Let me run to that store on the corner and pick up some ice cream for dessert.''

''That'll be fine.'' She felt much the same warm happiness as she had the day she had been accepted as a member of the orchestra. Yet this was a more exciting, dizzying feeling. She was glad to have a few minutes to collect herself and to run a comb through her hair when Ralph went off after the ice cream.

She'd intended to tell him about the man Ross had assigned to follow her. Suddenly it occurred to Nella to wonder whether Ross had meant everywhere. She had taken him to mean just while she was in the symphony hall. Was the little man outside now? She glanced at the street from a living room window. Nobody in sight. She must remember to mention him to Ralph when he got back.

Hearing his step on the stair, Nella started to meet him when the phone rang. As Ralph put his head around the door, she pulled a hideous face at him from the telephone. Lottie!

''Nella—Nella, you've got to talk to him right away! You've got to call and straighten him out! You'd never *believe* the way he talked to me this afternoon, keeping me after a two-rehearsal day and all that, and I *told* him I had to do some very important errands, but he just sits there like Buddha on a monument, he won't *listen* to any intelligent suggestions, you've got to call him!''

Deciding to let the implication slide, Nella said, ''Lottie, who—''

''And when I *told* him Freed was the one he ought to be questioning, you'll never guess what he said to me!

191

He said, when did I stop suspecting that Regal McCord was the killer! Well, I ask you! He couldn't be the killer if he got killed himself, could he? Any fool can see that!''

"Lottie, I—"

"Just because the other day I dropped him a little hint or two about Regal—and you know, yourself, how *funny* Regal had been acting—Nella, I know he thinks I had something to do with Regal's death! You've got to back me up. I told him how you and I and Zaidee had all talked it over and agreed about it the other day, you remember, don't you?''

"LOTTIE!" There was no other way to get her attention. Nella just bellowed her name and waited.

There was a startled pause, and finally a feeble, "What?"

"Look, Lottie, I have company right now, and anyway, you're too upset. I'm sure more than you really need to be. Lieutenant Ross has to talk to everybody. Why would he suspect you more than anyone else? Nobody knows exactly when Regal died, so I suppose nobody in the whole orchestra has an alibi. And—''

"That's just it." The pause had done Lottie good; she sounded much calmer now. "They said he was strangled sometime before eight in the morning. Ross was looking at my hands, and just because I'm a big woman, and tall—and Regal was such a wiry little thing, but you know, Nella, I couldn't—'' Her voice was edging up again, toward hysteria.

"Lottie, Lottie, calm down. Listen: you need to get into a good hot tub and soak till you're sleepy. Then take a couple of aspirin with some warm milk, and get yourself into bed. Your nerves are getting away with you, and this is no time for that to happen to any of us.''

She seemed to take real comfort in Nella's firm

assumption of control. "You're right, Nella. I'll do that, but tell me, what do you think . . ."

"I have company now, Lottie. See you at the concert tomorrow." She said good-bye quickly and hung up.

Ralph had her drink ready for her, and was halfway through the composition of an elegant green salad. "What do you think, ma'am: Doesn't this look delicious?"

"It'd better be delicious! That's my last avocado."

"The Lord loves a cheerful giver," he reminded her. "Who would you rather share your last avocado with?"

"Whom," she said automatically. "Well, now with Lottie Williams, poor thing. She was practically hysterical, trying to tell me that Lieutenant Ross has it in for her. She said he almost accused her of the murders."

"No way," Ralph said energetically. "That woman's too scatty to plan and carry out one murder, let alone two. Ross must have known that from the first day. Wonder what made her think he's after her? Did she say what he asked?"

"Not in detail. I gathered that Lottie took exception to the way he looked at her hands. And he was chiding her, I guess, about all the accusations she's been flinging around."

"Time somebody called her bluff," Ralph grumbled. "She's getting to be a menace. Did you hear her pitching into Nina Oldenberg at the break, suggesting she was 'behaving suspiciously' after the concert when she was backstage Tuesday night? No, come to think of it, you weren't around."

"Nina Oldenberg! How could she, in the first place, and why should she, in the second place? She *liked* Milton. She and her husband are putting up funds for an endowment in his name, don't forget."

"Well, come to think of it, I suppose she could have

done it, physically, as well as anybody. That is, she *was* backstage that night. Always with somebody, it seemed, but who's to say she didn't have five minutes between conversations? That's all she'd need; two or three minutes to get there and set it up, another minute or two to see him step into the lighted area and push it off.''

Nella said stubbornly, "But she *liked* Milton!"

Ralph said, "Hasn't it ever occurred to you, Nella, that this murder might have been a mistake? I mean, maybe the wrong victim? How many men are there in the orchestra, say, sixty? And every damn one of them in a tail suit and white tie. What's to prevent the murderer from thinking Milton's back is somebody else's?"

"Whose, for example?"

"Well, I know it's far-fetched, but I was thinking . . . maybe the victim was supposed to have been Lyle."

"Lyle! Why, he's much taller than Milton! And he was wearing a tux, not tails. And a *black* tie, not a white one. You know the League members always do."

"The main difference in that dim lighting, I'd think, would be the hair. Wavy gray instead of wavy brown. But suppose it didn't catch the light, or the murderer told himself that it didn't show gray because of the dim light. And the color of tie wouldn't make any difference, of course, with the back turned. Don't you see, if the murderer expected it to be Lyle, he'd explain away the differences to himself? Height, for example. People look taller in dark corners, don't they?"

"And the tails?"

"Say he could see, maybe, a gleam reflected from the satin lapel as his victim turned to the light. Would he also bother to check for tails, even if he could distinguish them in the dark? I'm inclined to believe he'd just say to himself, 'There he is!' and then—bam!"

She shivered. "It's horrible. I think of it constantly."

Ralph said, "What a fool I am! Forgive me, Nella."

"Oh, it's all right. We need to think about it, I guess, and try to figure out what happened the best we can . . . the note!" She turned to him, puzzled. "What about the note that Milton had? Why did he get it, if Lyle was supposed to be the victim?"

"Oh, I think Milton was supposed to receive the note, all right, and react just as he did—by going there," Ralph said.

"How? What do you mean?"

"Suppose something went wrong with the timing—that is, that the murder was supposed to happen first, and then Schring was to get there and discover the body."

"But the killer would know that—that the murder hadn't happened yet, when Milton showed up . . ."

"Not if he took Schring to be Lyle, and thought Schring would be along in a few minutes. To discover the body, don't you see, and with any luck, he might get blood on him, or do or say something that looked incriminating."

"But how was Lyle supposed to get there, if he didn't have the note?"

"Oh, any number of ways. How do we know he didn't have a direct communication with the murderer? Just flat an appointment to be on that spot, which he couldn't, or at least didn't, keep? I tell you, something has that man mighty worried these days. For an ex-athlete, he'd looking downright peaked. I think he's scared to death."

"Then why doesn't he tell Ross? If he knows all that, he could clear up this whole mess."

"The only reason I can see for his keeping still is that whatever he knows is damaging to him. Now, what do you suppose is so important to keep secret that he'll put up with murder to hide it?"

She said, "Well, let's think of all the possibilities."

"Nella. No." He smiled and laid a long index finger across her lips. "I'm crazy to be speculating like this. Too much imagination, is what my mother used to call it, when I thought up a different excuse every time I played hookey. Let's have a truce. No more talk. No more murder. No more mystery. Nobody here but Nella and Ralph. Okay?"

"Well . . ." Tears suddenly sprang into her eyes without her knowing whether they were from relief or frustration. Ralph leaned forward as if to see them better, and suddenly was kissing her firmly, for a long, long time.

Sometime later they rescued the meatloaf, which hadn't suffered greatly from its overheating, and the salad, only a little wilted. After the ice cream, Nella insisted on washing up immediately. She thought they could use a sobering interval. They agreed that it was too early for promises and that they must very sensibly go together for a while without commitment on either side. Get to know each other, in short.

When all the cleaning up was done, they practiced getting to know each other for a while, till Nella shooed him away for the night. Watching him climb down the stairs, she realized that she had completely forgotten to tell him about Ross's little man.

CHAPTER XIX

There was a policy the Symphony League tried to enforce: no rehearsals on concert Mondays. The same concert would be repeated the following day, Tuesday, and there always was a Tuesday morning rehearsal for the following week's program. But Monday mornings were kept for the musicians to rest and gather their artistic forces.

Most of the players took advantage of the chance to sleep late. Not, however, Angel Angelo. She rapped repeatedly on Nella's kitchen door. Getting no answer and finding it unlocked, she walked in and past a pile of dirty clothes heaped on the living room floor for sorting, to find Nella vacuuming under the bed.

"Nella—"

"Ahhhhgh! Oh my God, Angel! How you scared me!"

"Oh, I'm truly sorry. Your door was unlocked; you must have taken out the trash or something and left it unlatched. I heard the vacuum, so I came in. Knew you'd never hear me knocking."

Sitting on the floor, Nella smoothed her rumpled red hair with one hand. "What on earth brings you out so early?" she asked, hoping she didn't sound as cross as she felt.

Angel waved an airy hand. "Oh, I was just in the neighborhood, running some errands, and thought maybe we could have a cup of coffee together."

"There's a fresh pot in the kitchen. Let's do it."

Listening to Angel's high-pitched chatter while she

set out the coffee things, Nella wondered whether a man would find it more enchanting to wake up every morning to such a beautiful face, or more dreadful to hear that horrible whine first thing each day.

"If I asked you something, Nella, would you promise not to breathe a word about it to a soul?"

"I guess so unless I hear it from some other source as well, and find it needs to be discussed," Nella said carefully.

"Huh?"

"Oh, rats! I'm just saying, if I hear your secret, whatever it is, from somebody else, then I'll feel free to talk about it."

"You won't hear this from anybody else." Angel's lovely long lashes swept down and up. "You couldn't. I just thought it up."

Nella laughed.

After a minute, Angel saw the joke. "Oh, no. I don't mean I'm making up secrets to tell. I mean, I just figured out that maybe I ought to do this. Three or four of us have been saying what a shame it is, and somebody ought to do something about it, so I thought, being a wife and mother myself, maybe I should start a petition."

"About what?"

"Why, to ask the homosexuals to resign from the orchestra. You know, Pete Rollinson and Howard Freed."

"Why?"

"Why! You can't be—no, of course not. Well, you're not in *favor* of them, are you?" Angel's whine went higher in her indignation.

"They haven't asked for my opinion, so I haven't given it," Nella said. "But you have come here to ask my opinion, Angel, so I want to give it to you, as honestly as I can.

198

"I do think sex is an important issue for every human being. I think it's important what people do about it, and what they say about it. But I don't think it anywhere *near* as important as people pretend it is! I believe thousand of people have lived satisfying, wonderful lives without having any sex at all. I think anybody who wants to can do the very same thing today. I know a hundred years ago we were worse off, when you couldn't admit that sex even existed, much less that you were interested in it. Freud yanked us out of that trap, but he dumped us into a worse one, in my opinion. I am sick to death of all this palaver about sex! Even cats and dogs find other things to think about, occasionally!"

Nella drew in a long breath and had to remember not to smile as she saw Angel staring at her, round-eyed at her vehemence. I suppose I'm proving somebody-or-other's theory right now, she mused. Say "sex" to me and you get an emotional reaction. But there was one more thing she was determined to say.

"Most of all, I don't think you, or I, can judge other people's sexual conduct, and say, this one's right and that one's wrong. All I ask of homosexuals, or anybody else, is, just quit talking about it! Your sexual inclinations are none of my business. That's one thing I do feel sure about, with sex: it's private, or it ought to be! Now, Angel, don't you realize that Freed and Pete are just none of our business? And don't you appreciate their discretion? Have they ever bothered you about it? Of course not! And they won't. Besides, you know they're not the only ones in the orchestra. I am aware of four or five more people in that category, none of whom bother me in the least. So why should they bother you?"

Angel batted her lashes. "Well, all right. I really don't know if I'll get up a petition, actually. If that's the way people feel about it. Anyway, really I was wondering about something else. Have you thought about these murders?''

How do you answer a question like that, Nella wondered. Would it be better to say, ''Why, no I haven't given them a thought,'' or ''Yes, constantly,'' or what?

Angel was going on: ''I mean, today makes a week since Milton died, you know. And it looks to me as if Lieutenant Ross is just as baffled as he was the first day, don't you think?''

''Why, I can't tell. He doesn't give anything away. Do you have any ideas?'' It was becoming obvious to Nella as she asked that here was the real reason for Angel's early-morning call. She had tested out the petition idea on Nella; now she would test her crime theories.

Angel said, ''Well, as a matter of fact, I was wondering whether he knows about Nina Oldenberg.''

''What about her?'' I know where this is coming from, Nella thought. Lottie Williams, you have a lot to answer for.

''Why, that she was in love with Milton. Didn't you know? The other night at Bilbo's, when she started to tell me about the Fund, there were real tears in her eyes. I saw them myself. I'd always suspected they were having an affair . . . sometime last year, wasn't it? Oh, you weren't in the Orchestra then.''

''But if she really loved Milton, she wouldn't have killed him even if he'd gotten tired of her, would she? Because she could always hope he'd come back to her.''

''Oh, I don't think so, not for a minute. But there's her husband, isn't there; suppose he really cares for her. He can't stop her romancing around, because she's got plenty of moneybags of her own and doesn't need him, so . . .''

''You mean, he might have killed Milton out of

200

jealousy?''

Angel said, practically, "Well, maybe it was the only thing he *could* do."

When Angel left, Nella fell into a fury of house-cleaning. She made it and her trips to the laundromat last all day, topping off the work by polishing the silver. Then it was time for bathing, dressing, and driving to the hall for the concert.

Derek John, dependably, had settled down and led the orchestra through a workmanlike performance. It wasn't inspired, but it was adequate, and the applause that greeted the last note was generous.

Peering into the audience, Nella couldn't see a vacant chair anywhere in the hall. The murders, apparently, had swelled the usual crowd to capacity. She glanced at the Oldenbergs' box to the right of center, and then remembered that they were Tuesday ticketholders.

Backstage, Ralph gave her arm a welcoming squeeze. "May I follow you home tonight?"

"No, thanks, Ralph. I've worked like a madwoman all day. I'm going straight home and zonk out, to be ready for rehearsal tomorrow."

"Be careful, then. See you in the morning."

When he saw him again before rehearsal Tuesday morning, Ralph remembered having noticed before the little man who had followed Nella. Ralph was new enough to the orchestra so that he didn't trust himself to recognize by sight all ninety-odd of the musicians. He couldn't be sure but was this some back-of-the-section player whom he just hadn't noticed before? He decided to say nothing till he could be positive the man didn't belong. As soon as rehearsal began, Ralph scanned all the players carefully. Couple of string players out, ill; their chairs were left vacant. A bass player was missing also. Ralph knew all the missing musicians. Among those present there was no little man. He was not, therefore, one of the orchestra.

When the Old Man nodded a gruff dismissal for the midmorning coffee break and stepped down, Ralph snapped his horn into its case and sat ready to take off after Nella.

She was taking her time, swabbing her instrument. "I won't see you at coffee break," she had already told him. "I still have to return that dratted music from the other day. I was so rattled at the time that I carried it right back upstairs with me. It's been stashed in my locker ever since."

Finally she moved, the neat little rectangular case in hand. She also had the sheaf of music. It was a wonder old Pritchett had not been calling her at home for the return of the music, she thought. He had probably been distracted because Ross had included Pritchett in his investigation this time.

They were here again this morning, but had not started calling for musicians as far as Nella knew. They were taking the stagehands first this time, perhaps because they could be presumed to know more about Regal, his sayings and doings.

There was an elevator that ran up to all levels and down to the basements, and a freight elevator, enormous, for sets and heavy equipment, but nobody used them. Especially today, Nella thought, I'm taking the stairs to be darn sure my little man stays right with me.

Wanting to make certain he wouldn't lose track of her, Nella had purposely said to Zaidee that she was returning music to the library after rehearsal. She had flashed a glance at her follower, and been rewarded by the tiniest of nods. With vast reassurance, she spotted him in a mirror on the light panel as she went to the stairs nearby. Nothing in the world to be nervous about now, she told herself; my own policeman's right behind me.

Chatting idly with Regal's replacement at the light panel, Ralph saw her start down. In a minute, sure enough, the little man came after. Ralph caught the stair door before it could close and slipped through.

The door at the landing was just swinging shut after Nella. The little man was halfway down the stairs. He looked back, surprised, over his shoulder. Reading the menace on Ralph's face, he ran down to the landing and turned. His hand was in his pocket. He crouched, professionally, coolly waiting.

Ralph did the one thing the policeman's training had not prepared him to meet. He fell on him. The stairs were steep and not very familiar to Ralph. Angry and in a hurry, he stubbed a toe, misjudged his recovery, and rocketed down on the little man. When Ralph disentangled himself, he found the little fellow stone cold unconscious. His head had struck hard on the landing door.

It made a dilemma for Ralph, who had been considerably jolted himself by the fall. Should he go on after Nella, or go back for help for this guy? Never mind following her now, he told himself. Nella would be all right on her own, with this sinister character off her trail. Ralph trudged back up the stairs to get help for the man.

Long, blank corridors stretched gloomily before Nella, as they had two days before. She should have made herself go back over this route that same day, Nella thought now, pushing down the rising, unreasoning dread inside her. She *had* to be able to get to the library when she needed to!

Oh, if they would only shut all the doors, get rid of all these black gaps along the way! It was a physical impossibility to keep her eyes from turning to peep at them fearfully as she passed each one. Nella walked along swiftly, thinking how skillful her guardian angel was showing himself to be. He'd made noise enough, though, a few minutes ago. It had almost sounded as if he had fallen down some of the steps, but now she couldn't hear a single footstep behind her.

She wouldn't for the world embarrass him by looking around, but it was a great comfort to know he was there. Otherwise, this deserted part of the building with its dim hall lights would be too spooky.

After the other day, the worst part was passing the black silences beyond the open doors. So easy to imagine somebody lurking just inside the shadows each time. There was another one ahead, on her left. She could even imagine that the shadow had moved. Nella couldn't help it. She must glance around for her guardian . . . .

Nobody. She was alone in this endless, dim hall. With the gaping door just ahead.

Where the shadow *had* moved . . . .

CHAPTER XX

Upstairs, Ralph wobbled along backstage to Lyle's office door. It was shut and, to his surprise, locked, though light shone through the opaque glass. He knocked loudly.

Nothing. He knocked again. An irate bellow, "Just a *minute*!" came through the door. Ralph had raised his hand to knock a third time when Sergeant Able ran up from the other direction.

"What's the matter, Mr. Payton? Have an accident? You don't look so good."

That was probably putting it mildly, Ralph knew, though he couldn't see for himself the darkening bruise on his cheek nor the wild mop of hair he hadn't thought to smooth. He gasped, "I've got the killer!"

Sergeant Able tried to look believing, but his answer gave him away: "Well, guess we'd better wait for the lieutenant. He's on the telephone to the chief right now. Liable to be a long call, and it's strictly private, so he locked the door. Want to sit down? I'll get you a chair."

Ralph stood up straight and forced his breathing to slow. "You don't seem to understand, Sergeant. I've knocked out a man downstairs, and I'm pretty sure he's our murderer."

"My God! Who is he?"

"Never saw him before—I mean, I *did* see him before, following Nella. Miss Payne. So I figured, he wasn't doing that for any good reason. Caught him following her downstairs just now. He's unconscious down there.''

It sounded pretty logical to Able, who hadn't been informed about Nella's bodyguard. "Let's go see."

As he and Ralph rounded the horseshoe curve going toward the left-hand end and went out of sight, Ross came to the door and opened it. Looking out, he noticed Nina Oldenberg approaching from the right-hand side. "Lieutenant Ross! Please! I must see you."

Her thick, dark hair looked even more attractive windblown and forgotten than when she remembered to comb it to perfection. Her cheeks were flushed, from excitement it seemed, and her eyes glittered nervously.

Ross said, "Come in," and shut the door behind her.

"I am being blackmailed," Nina Oldenberg said, not bothering to sit down.

Ross's astonishment did away with his tact. What kind of secret would this notorious woman pay to conceal? Truly baffled, he asked, "About what?"

She laughed shortly. "You've been hearing about my reputation," she said shrewdly, "that there is nothing I care about enough to hide. Well, that's just about right. But I do care about my—friends, who may have a greater need than I do, to be discreet. To be more exact, I should have said someone is *trying* to blackmail me. I told him to go to hell, but that was for psychological effect. I intend to see that he doesn't spread his glad tidings, somehow. That's why I'm here."

Ross waved at the leather chair. "Let's sit down and see if we can sort this out, Mrs. Oldenberg," he invited.

There was a pounding on the door, which Ross had inadvertently left on automatic lock. He strode to it now, jerked it open. "I'm busy," he growled. "What is it, Able?"

"Tim Connell. Payton knocked him out on the stairs. Said he was following Miss Payton. Anyway, we've hauled him up here, still out cold."

"Damn right he was following Miss Payne!" yelled Ross. "That was his assignment! Where's that fool Payton? I've got a good mind to arrest him for obstructing justice!"

Forgetting Nina Oldenberg entirely, Ross ran down the hall toward the light panel. Stretched on the floor in the wide area nearby lay the little man who had followed Nella. He was stirring, putting a hand to a head that obviously ached.

"Wait, Lieutenant. You mean, you *wanted* him to follow Nella?" Ralph asked. "He was guarding her?"

Ross nodded impatiently, peering into Connell's face. "He'll come around in a minute," he said.

"Then we can't wait! Come on—Nella's down there by herself!" Ralph shouted.

"Down where?" Ross asked.

"Two floors down—going to the library," groaned Ralph. "If the killer wants to get her—as you seem to think—he's got his best chance right now. Let's go!"

Leaving Connell to the ministrations of several stagehands and musicians who had gathered, the three of them ran.

Nina Oldenberg was in no mood to be stashed in an office and told to wait. She had nerved herself to face some very unpleasant possibilities, and she wanted to get the job done. When Lieutenant Ross rushed out, she fished out a cigarette, lighted it, and paced the office a few times. She had just squashed the cigarette and taken a step toward the door when it slowly opened. In a moment she saw that it was being pushed by an ebony walking stick that glittered at the neck. In the next moment, Verna Smallwood took a precarious step into the room.

"Thank you, Jimmie," she said to the uniformed driver behind her. "Please wait for me outside for a while." Having shut the door with meticulous care, she turned and surveyed Nina for a long minute.

"You are Mrs. Oldenberg, aren't you?" she asked. "I am Verna Smallwood. We've been introduced once or twice at Symphony League meetings, have we not? And of course I've known Julius all his life."

"That's right, Mrs. Smallwood. We've been introduced a few times. It's nice to see that you're well again," Nina said pleasantly. The old lady reminded her of her grandmother, who had lived and died in their home before Nina's family had come into their era of prosperity.

"May I ask, my dear—I have a reason—if you have come here to discuss this murder business?"

It didn't occur to Nina to resent the question, any more than if it had been her grandmother asking. She looked into the glittering dark eyes and away. She felt a blush rising. "I think so. I mean, I'm afraid there's a connection between—between certain things I want to tell the policeman about, and the murder. I'm afraid so."

Mrs. Smallwood tottered closer, laid a brown hand on Nina's arm. My dear girl, you have been rather foolish, haven't you?" she asked gently. "Come and sit down here, beside me." She pulled Nina toward the sofa.

"Sometimes young women like you get into mischief, more than they ever meant to, just because they have nothing useful to do with their time. What you need, I believe, is some nice club you could get interested in. Not a silly one, you understand, but one that does some good in the world. For example, the Antares Club."

The Antares Club! Only the cream of the social scene belonged to that prestigious group. It never made the papers as far as the social columns went; none of its members desired the publicity. But its charitable work was famous all over the nation.

"Well, we may talk about that later," Verna Smallwood went on. "Right now, please, tell me all about it, dear. It may be that I can help, and in any case, you'll feel better for having someone to confide in."

How long had Nella been standing still? Afraid to go on, afraid to go back. Well, she had to do something. She groped in her purse for the little Mace pen she carried on night jobs. Pencil, ballpoint, pencil. Not there. Must have left it in the black purse.

Footsteps: light and stealthy? Coming from around the bend ahead, from the direction of the music library. As they grew louder, they pounded more threateningly into Nella's mind. She forgot about the moving shadow. She jumped into the dark doorway, shrank back into the dark.

It was Manning, his oiled black hair catching the light. He was walking along quickly, looking around warily. Looking for her? He had been there when she'd taken the music out of her locker this morning, must have heard her saying, for the little man to hear, that she would have to return it. Was he afraid she might have seen him disposing of Schring, whom he'd been unable to fire? In spite of Ralph's ideas, had Manning's steadily, stealthily accumulated power over people's lives finally turned his brain?

She held her breath. Then she bent down, took off her shoes. Hose would tear on the rough concrete floor, but they'd make no noise.

Manning was passing the door. Making up her mind to cound to ten before she slipped out, Nella took another step back into the room. She was holding her music in the bend of her left elbow and her instrument and the shoes in her left hand. Automatically, her right hand went into the darkness behind her, warding off obstacles.

Suddenly her hand closed on familiar objects. For a second her brain refused to acknowledge the known, the familiar, in this wrong blackness. Then she knew what she was holding in her right hand. Fingers.

I'm insane, she thought. I'm the crazy one. I'm finding Regal, again. I've gone out of my mind, and I have to keep finding him, over and over and . . . no. Not Regal.

It was not reason that told her this, but the feeling part of her. How do you know? Some portion of her mind asked, and the answer came without reflection. *This one is warm*. Alive!

As she thought, Nella flashed out of the room, around the last corner, and flew for the library door at the end of the hall.

Footsteps. Loud footsteps! How could she be making so much noise with her shoes off? She wasn't. They were behind her, running, retreating. She had a crazed vision of Regal, tongue lolling, eyes like saucers, running from the dark room. There was a shout. She didn't stop.

The library door flew open. Bilbo Jones dashed past, almost knocking her down. Nella stopped, looking into sanctuary, trying to interpret the sounds from around the last bend. Deaf old Pritchett was furious, babbling something about the music, about Bilbo. No time for that now. Nella threw her stack of music down anywhere and went out into the hall again. There was a regular babble of voices now. When she heard Ralph's, Nella ran forward.

Quite a crowd had gathered in the hall about fifty feet from the other side of the door where the shadow had moved. Bilbo and Bill Buskirk, one on each side, held a red-faced, maniacal stranger. It took Nella a long stare to recognize him as Robert Z. Lyle.

Sergeant Able, behind Lyle, was struggling to fasten handcuffs on him while he lunged around, cursing at Manning, who was sitting on the floor.

Hanks of silver hair framed a face that twisted with rage and hate. Lyle was drawing rasping breaths like a man in convulsions. Below the steel cuffs, his hands still clutched and clawed.

Manning was nursing his neck tenderly and trying to say something to Ross. He seemed unconscious of the torn white paper in his hand until Ross twitched it out of his grasp and put it carefully into a pocket. Ralph was pulling at Ross's sleeve, yelling that they had to find Nella, they had to find Nella. When Nella reached him, she had to poke him to get his attention.

"Oh, Nella!" He took her into his arms and almost crushed out her breath. It would have been embarrassing, except that nobody was paying them the slightest attention.

For a long time she stood in his arms, letting him squeeze away the terror, the shock, the panic. Afterwards, when she tried to remember what it was that he stood murmuring in her ear, she only knew it had been tender and protecting and infinitely healing. After a while they noticed that the babble had died down and drew apart to look around. There was a chuckle. Bilbo was the only one still there. "Come on, Love's Young Dreamers, let's get out of here!"

He led the way.

CHAPTER XXI

Ross was explanatory later in the Mauve Room where Bill, Zaidee, and Ralph and Nella followed him and Bilbo. He said he guessed they deserved to hear the details.

First, he apologized to Nella for not knowing right away that her guardian had—he glanced wryly at Ralph —met with an accident. "I was tied up, talking to the chief on the phone," he explained. "Had the door locked. By the time Bright Boy, here, got the news to me that he'd cut off your protection, you could've been strangled yourself."

"I thought he was the murderer," Ralph said. "It was the second day I'd seen him trailing Nell. And even the first time, his face looked vaguely familiar to me. First I checked and made sure he didn't belong in the orchestra. Then, what was I supposed to think? I *knew* I'd seen that guy around here before."

"Of course you have, you damned fool," growled Ross. "He's one of my uniformed men—came here the first night we were called."

"That's it—he stood just inside the stage door!" Ralph slapped his brow, hit a bruise, and winced. "I'd never have made the connection from seeing him in plain clothes!"

"I kept meaning to tell you about him," Nella mourned. "Somehow I just never got a chance."

Ralph said, "Anyway, I'm mortified about knocking out your protector. But how was I to know that was Ross's man? I wasn't going to have anybody stalking you!"

Ross said, "Tim's a little mortified himself, letting you knock him out that way. Jackass claims you *fell* on him!"

"As a matter of fact, I did," Ralph admitted. "Lucky for me, I guess. A trained officer like him would probably have knocked *me* out, otherwise."

Nella prompted, "And then you couldn't leave him there, not knowing how badly he was hurt . . ."

". . . And I thought the danger to you was taken care of. Took a while before we got him up and comfortable and had enough explanations to realize you were down there, alone."

"Not alone enough," Nella said. "Lyle was hiding in that prop room, behind the door. I forgot all about seeing something move, and ducked in there when I heard someone—it was Manning, coming from the library.

"When I moved back, getting out of Manning's line of vision, my hand touched his and all I could think of was poor Regal, somehow standing there, staring . . ." Her flesh crawled as she remembered her hand closing on that living hand in the dark room. "He could have strangled me, easily. Why—why didn't he do it while he had the chance?"

"He had a tough choice to make. He was waiting down there for Manning to come back from the library. There was a piece of evidence that Manning had hidden down there, and Lyle meant to get it, and him, once and for all.

"Manning laid himself open to attack, in a way. You see, he can't stand to be treated like one of the musicians; he likes preferential service. So he phoned Pritchett from upstairs, to tell him he was on the way down, and wanted one certain piece of music to be ready. You have to speak pretty loudly for old Pritchett to hear on the phone, it seems, and Lyle overheard and made his plan accordingly. Then you came tripping along; another party he wanted removed from the scene. Which to choose? I think he figured to kill Manning first and catch you on the way back.

"Of course, if you'd happened to run the other way—back to the stairs—he would've had to kill you then and there. It would have been easy for him to catch you. He keeps in shape; jogs every day. Took him just a few steps to get to Manning. That bird's lucky we weren't any slower than we were, getting down to the basement. He'll have some bruises on his throat for a long while, anyway."

"What in the world did Lyle have against Manning?" Zaidee wanted to know. "All the rest of us had reason to hate Oscar more. He could pull strings and cut off our extra jobs, or just generally make our lives miserable; but what could he do to Lyle?"

"That's a long story . . ." Ross began, stopping to listen as Sergeant Able came in and murmured to him.

"Oh, my God, I'd forgotten all about her! *Both* of them? Well, put them in the yellow dressing room, please," he said. "I'm coming right now." He rose to go out.

Zaidee cried, "That's not fair! You haven't explained anything yet!"

Ross's green eyes could twinkle, and now they did. "Tell you what I'll do," he said. "You all certainly deserve a decent explanation. I'll make sure Buskirk, here, has the whole story. Then you can have a regular gathering and worm it all out of him at your leisure."

Leisure—"My God, rehearsal!" groaned Bilbo.

Lottie Williams came in the open door. "It occurred to me you'd like to know," she said primly, "that the Old Man has cancelled the other half of today's rehearsal. He had a tantrum first, but the lieutenant convinced him to do it. What we'll do is make it up tomorrow afternoon. Except for the concert tonight, we're all free until then."

214

Lottie sat down in a vacant chair. Plainly she had heard the lieutenant's remark about having a gathering for further explanations, and she meant to be included.

Bilbo saw his duty and he did it. "Let's meet at my house tomorrow evening," he said. "Billie'll kill me if she misses out on the explanations. Can you make it, Bill, say around eight? Good. Then, everybody come and hear the story."

Nella asked Zaidee, "Who do you suppose are the people Ross is seeing in the yellow dressing room? Someone to do with all this?"

"Two of them," Lottie said. "It's Nina Oldenberg herself, looking like the wrath of God. She hasn't even combed her hair, let alone put on any makeup!"

"But why . . ." Zaidee began, and stopped of her own accord. "Well, he said it was a long story. I guess we'll get the facts tomorrow night."

"You haven't asked who the other woman is," Lottie complained. "Would you believe it's Mrs. Verna Smallwood?"

"No! She's not even supposed to leave home yet!"

"Well, she came to the concert last week, and she went to Milton's funeral, and now she's here. When all that commotion started downstairs and she found out the killer was Lyle, she phoned some of the Board members and got an emergency ruling for the Old Man to carry on alone till they can meet. She's in there with Ross and Mrs. Oldenberg, right now."

It seemed incredible that they should then go tamely home and, in the evening, come back prepared to play; but, of course, that is exactly what happened. They congregated backstage before the performance just as they had the night Milton Schring had died.

215

CHAPTER XXII

Ralph came by for Nella at a quarter to eight the next night. He complimented her on the lime-green pantsuit she wore.

Thanking him, Nella said, "I made sure to wear something comfortable. I intend to sit there until I understand every last detail!"

Billie Jean and Bilbo, like their company, were subdued. Angel and Lottie had come together. The Buskirks were there, along with five or six musicians Nella and Ralph knew only slightly, and—to Nella's surprise—Sergeant Able.

Billie Jean whispered, "Isn't he cute? He says he came to listen and learn. Personally, I think he's smitten with that blonde flute player—Bonnie, is it? Over there by the armchair."

"Simmer down, Matchmaker, and let Buskirk get started," Bilbo said.

Bill began where Ross had left off the day before. "It's as the lieutenant said, a long story," he said. "You might call it a love story, in a way. It started last year, when Mrs. Nina Oldenberg and Milton Schring got involved in an affair; not a new situation, I understand, for either one of them."

"You can say that again," Lottie said. "That female's strictly the love-'em-and-leave-'em type. Always has been."

"So was Milton Schring," Buskirk went on. "But this time, to her own surprise, Mrs. Oldenberg found herself deeply in love. That's what she came to tell Lieutenant Ross yesterday. She feels responsible for starting a chain of events that finally led to murder, and she decided to come down and tell us everything she could. She said when she found Schring was getting tired of their romance, she started a flirtation with Lyle, trying to revive Schring's interest.

"There was no problem about keeping her romances from her husband, poor thing. He's used to ignoring them by now. But Robert Lyle's wife was another matter. She controls Lyle by controlling his money supply. Lyle was terrified that Helene would find out he was courting Nina Oldenberg. At the same time, the poor devil was head over heels crazy about Mrs. O."

"I've always said it," Angel said. "This orchestra is nothing but woman-chasers! There's two right there: Schring and Lyle. And Oscar Manning makes three."

"Not in this situation," Buskirk said. "Manning came into it quite by accident, and he wasn't interested in the gorgeous Nina at all, once he found out she couldn't be blackmailed.

"Of course, Lyle soon got to be a pest as far as Nina was concerned. She'd never meant for him to get so deeply involved. She finally wrote to him and told him in very plain terms to leave her alone or she would have a chat with his wife. Not really wanting to get him into trouble at home, she mailed the letter to him at the concert hall. It got to the hall all right, but into Manning's hands. He says he slit it open by mistake, when it was in the batch with his own mail. That may be so; but it was marked "Personal" and addressed to "Mr. Robert Z. Lyle" individually and not as League president. Anyway, once Manning had read the letter, he had Lyle by the short hairs.

Manning's a manipulator. He doesn't need money; he makes all he wants. What he needs, and will do anything to get, is power. He started out small with Lyle. At first, he didn't say what proof of the affair he had; just let Lyle know that he, Manning, was aware of Lyle's interest in Mrs. Oldenberg. Then he'd ask for a small favor. Little things at first, then bigger ones.''

"Like promoting Freed to solo chair," Nella said. "Was that just testing his strength with Lyle, then?"

"Say it was killing three birds with one stone. He'd prove his power, he'd have another musician under obligations to him, and he'd also have the pleasure of putting down, or getting entirely rid of, Schring, whom he detested."

Billie Jean said, "Of course Oscar detested Milton. He couldn't bully him and he couldn't compete with him when it came to women. But has Oscar been admitting all this about blackmailing Lyle and trying to blackmail Nina?"

"No, no. He's clammed up entirely, on the advice of his lawyer. Likely to stay that way, too. It's Nina Oldenberg and Robert Lyle who've been talking."

"Doesn't Lyle have a lawyer? Hasn't he advised Lyle not to talk?" Bilbo asked.

"Oh, yes. Soon as Lyle calmed down and started thinking, he called an attorney. Luckily for us, he'd been talking his head off and pretty well covered the subject while he was still in a rage. It's going to be mighty hard for him to backtrack on everything he's told us."

"Go on," Zaidee said. "Manning was blackmailing Lyle. Lyle was in love with Nina, and Nina wanted Schring . . . oh! Is that why Lyle murdered Schring?"

"He said not," Buskirk said. "He claims it was a mistake. He says Schring's coat was tossed onto Manning's hook, and he had meant to slip the note asking for a meeting into Manning's pocket. He set up the booby trap while the concert was going on, and slipped out of the Mauve Room while Trevelyn was in the bathroom and konked Schring, thinking it was Manning."

"I suppose it could happen that way," Ralph said. "They're about the same weight, and not more than a couple of inches different in height."

"Freud says there are no mistakes," Bilbo said. "When Schring died, Lyle was rid of a successful rival. Makes you wonder, doesn't it?"

"We may never know for sure which way it was," Bill said. "I suspect we've gotten our last word out of Lyle, now that his attorney's on the scene."

"But think what a hellish shock it must have been," Zaidee said. "There he was thinking Manning was dead, and they come to tell him Schring has been killed."

"Oh—I remember something Regal said," Nella said. "That Lyle had to ask him twice, to understand who had died. Regal thought it showed how little he cared about the musicians."

"But Freed," Lottie said, "why was Freed acting so peculiar if he had nothing to do with all of this?"

When nobody answered her question, Lottie added, "Well I think it was mighty queer!"

"Exactly," Buskirk said. "But the person who really acted peculiar was McCord, and he paid for it. He learned or guessed about the coat hook business. Probably he eavesdropped on every two people he found talking. He looked up the hook owners on his list—and then said he'd lost the list when the lieutenant asked him to produce it."

Ralph asked, "Did you ever find the list?"

"No, but we can do without it if necessary. We've located the hook users on either side of Schring and Manning—and don't forget, Manning had two or three reserved there for his use. If we have to, we can use people's testimony about who were assigned to the neighboring hooks. They will have noticed, and remembered, Manning's having more than his share."

"Was that list what Manning's office was searched

for?'' Angel asked.

"I think not; more likely it was for Nina Oldenberg's letter to Lyle. When Lyle began to buck against things that Manning wanted him to do, Manning finally came right out and told Lyle he had the letter—even taunted him with the fact that it was in the building, but where Lyle would never find it. We figure that's when Lyle decided that Manning should die. He didn't much care just when it happened. Said his main idea was to choose a time and a method when there'd be a maximum of suspects. At that, it took him so long to get Trevelyn out of circulation, and get himself a minute to run around and do the job, that more people had gone home than he'd counted on."

"It's too tricky," Zaidee said. "What if Milton hadn't happened to step out into the exact spot just then? Lyle would have had to get back to Trevelyn fast, or he'd have started wondering what was happening."

"It didn't matter what Trevelyn thought," Bill said. "His driver was due to take him to the airport at any moment. If he'd come out of the bathroom and found Lyle missing, and had to leave without seeing him again, he might have considered it a little rude, but he surely wouldn't have delayed an international flight to hunt for Lyle to say good-bye."

"Let's get back to Regal," Nella said worriedly. "I just don't see why Lyle had to kill him."

"I hadn't finished his story," Buskirk said. "When he saw how Schring's and Manning's coats could have been mixed up, he always remembered hearing a scene where Manning was taunting Lyle about that letter. It took him a while—he was pretty slow in the head—but he finally put it together. He went to Lyle pretending to know more than he really did, and tried a shakedown."

"Oh! I heard that. I mean," Lottie explained hastily, "I heard Regal on the phone, saying, 'the truth about

Schring,' and 'I'll meet you down there,' but I thought he was *being* blackmailed, he sounded so mad!"

"His form of bluster, I guess," Bill said. "Proving he wasn't scared. Poor fool, he ought to have been. He headed down for the library where they were supposed to meet, early that morning, and Lyle just popped out of that room and zapped him."

Zaidee shuddered. "He should have remembered that Lyle was quite a well-known athlete in his college days. I guess it was no trick for him to strangle the little fellow."

Billie Jean said, "Wasn't he taking an awful chance? Surely any of the musicians or stagehands who saw him around that early would think it was mighty odd."

Ralph said, "I guess he must have been careful to lock the door behind him when he came in—Regal normally left it open, and so did whoever got there first. Finding it locked, old Prichett would think himself the first one to arrive, as usual, and go about his business."

"And that place is one monstrous barn," Bilbo added. "I can't think of anyplace so easy to hide in. You could have an army in there without anybody's knowing it. All he had to do was to dodge upstairs before anybody else came in. Then he had a choice of hiding places. Could even have gone into his own office and taken a nap. Maybe he did."

Nella asked, "Why hasn't Oscar Manning been scared all this time? It seems to me he's been remarkably cool about these murders. The only thing that really seemed to bother him was having his office torn up. It's hard to imagine he's that brave."

Buskirk said, "The lieutenant says Manning's so conceited that he really couldn't believe anyone would want to kill him. It was easier for him to think it was some private enemy of Schring's, and he did think so.

"When his office was burglarized, though, he had to

realize that Lyle was on the warpath, looking for that letter. It may be that even after McCord's death, the only connection Manning could see was that Lyle was using the confusion over the murders to make his search."

"Where was the letter, anyway?" Nella asked. "If it had been in Manning's office, Lyle would have found it. Every piece of paper there had been gone over."

"It was in a really safe place," Buskirk said. "In a music folder. Pritchett clued me to that; Manning came in and asked for some obscure score last week. Studied it over for a short time, and then handed it back, saying that it wasn't what he wanted after all. Tuesday he ran down there again and asked for the same score. Carried it over to a table for a few minutes, then said no, it still wouldn't do, and handed it back. Had old Pritchett biting nails, but what did that matter to Manning?"

Billie Jean said, "He must have thought, after his office was ransacked, that he'd better put the thing in a bank box or somewhere out of the building, at any rate. Did he say?"

"He's not talking," Bill said. "Both from choice, and because he's got a mighty sore throat. Lyle was hoping he'd go after the letter, and had followed him on purpose. He could have finished Manning off easily in another couple of minutes. Then he could have hidden again and waited for Nella to come out of the library."

"But I wouldn't have—I'd felt those fingers!" Nella said. "I'd have made Pritchett come with me, or phoned upstairs."

"Oh, you did? Then he must have known that. But suppose, after he's killed Manning and stashed him in a side room, he'd just boldly walked into the library and demanded to know what was going on; claimed he'd heard running footsteps and had to come to see what was the matter. Wouldn't you have felt safe to go back with him?"

She said slowly, "Well, yes, I would. And Pritchett, very likely, wouldn't hear or understand a word we said to each other."

"Fortunately, it happened that Bilbo was in the library. He heard the scuffling and rushed to the rescue. Managed to hold Lyle off Manning till we got there."

"I couldn't keep a grip on him. He was just plain out of his skull," Bilbo said.

Bill said, "Frustration hits some people that way. He'll calm down. He'll get the best lawyers money can buy. What do you wanta bet, he'll get off with a hung jury, or not sufficient evidence?"

Bilbo said, "Maybe so, on the murder. *If* Mrs. Lyle decides to stand by him. But the letter; you've got that, haven't you? That's enough to force his resignation as president of the Symphony League. We'll be through with him, at any rate."

"Well . . . about that letter," Bill said slowly, "I believe that's been returned to the original sender. Part of a negotiated settlement, you might say," he grinned.

"You must have noticed that little Mrs. Smallwood had made another trip to the hall, against her doctor's orders, last Tuesday morning? She's been worried to death by all the newspapers: Regal's death, the burglary, and of course, Milton Schring's death. She came to jog us up. We weren't making enough progress.

"Well, the lieutenant got called downstairs before he even knew she was in the building. She came into his office—Lyle's, I should say—and found Nina Oldenberg, who had come meaning to give herself away as little as possible, but to put Ross onto the fact that Manning was a blackmailer."

Buskirk smiled at his sister. "Zee's always telling me what a little champion the old gal is," he said. "Now I believe it. She took to Mrs. O. right away. Persuaded her to tell the whole truth so's to help get things cleared up. She's going to take Nina under her wing socially, it seems. Don't know how that'll work out, but it should be interesting as hell to watch.''

Sergeant Able, securely ensconced in the corner with the interesting little flute player, unexpectedly piped up. ''Don't worry about Lyle any more. The Oldenbergs are definitely going to see to it that his connection with the Symphony is over.''

''Manning's, too,'' Zaidee put in. ''Best thing for him to do after this is to leave town. Let him try New York or L.A.—he's always bragging about his connections there.''

''Thank God he'll be going,'' sighed Lottie. ''He'd never have forgiven me for that closet episode, not if I'd lived to be a hundred.''

Zaidee said, ''The one I'm sorry for is Nina Oldenberg. She really did care for Milton, but he got tired of her.''

''Don't pity her too much,'' Billie Jean advised. ''Mr. Oldenberg's taking her on a three-month tour of the Greek Islands, borrowing a yacht for it; just to get all this off her mind. I could do a lot of forgetting in three months in Greece!''

''Doing all right where you are,'' Bilbo growled. ''We ran out of cookies half an hour ago.''

''Never mind on our account,'' Nella said, standing up. ''Ralph and I need to be going. And tomorrow, I'm going back to the music library and sort out that folder I dropped, or old Pritchett will never let me hear the end of it.'' She was thinking, if I don't make myself go through that hall again right away, I may never be able to face it in the future.

''That's right, Nella,'' Ralph said gently. He pushed back his chair and brought her coat. ''I'll be going there with you, of course. It's a terrible burden,'' he told everyone gravely, ''to have a girl you can't even trust to go to the library by herself!''